WS

Hopson
High saddle

3919891
14.95
Apr94

DATE DUE			
26 '94			
JY1 1 '94			
JY2 6 '94			
MR 3 '95			
AP 6 '95			

GREAT RIVER REGIONAL LIBRARY

St. Cloud, Minnesota 56301

GAYLORD MG

HIGH SADDLE

Who was the stranger riding into town alone? He was hard, cold, spoke only a little and when he did, they wondered about his strange accent. The questions he asked chilled the townspeople.

Was he a bounty hunter, tracking down his prey with quiet cunning? Or a man with a memory which he would not allow to touch him? He cared for no human being, it seemed. Had the Apaches seen to that?

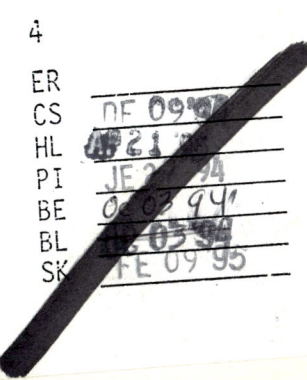

HIGH SADDLE

William Hopson

WESTERNS

First published 1952
by Arcadia House

This hardback edition 1993
by Chivers Press
by arrangement with
Donald MacCampbell Inc.

ISBN 0 7451 4562 0

Copyright © 1952 by Arcadia House
All rights reserved

British Library Cataloguing in Publication Data available

Printed and bound in Great Britain by
Redwood Press Limited, Melksham, Wiltshire

HIGH SADDLE

Chapter 1

THEY HAD told him in Holbrook not to try it; that a man was a plain damned fool to try it alone through Apache-infested country to the south. Nino was out with his band, raiding and slashing at ranches, wagon trains, and not even averse to slugging it out with the soldiers when the odds were anywhere near even. He was pretty young to hold such a high position as a raider—about twenty-eight, the same age as Cogin—but the hard-riding troopers had been finding out to their chagrin that as a leader Nino had few equals.

He hated the White Eyes as few Apaches hated them, because scalp hunters had killed his mother for the Mexican gold paid for her hair, and one of the White Eyes soldiers had shot Nino's brother in a skirmish.

But to the well meant advice Cogin paid no heed. His man was only a day or two ahead of him, and the trail had been a long one. All the way from Kansas, through the Indian Nation country to Texas, and thence across New Mexico Territory to the blistering heat of the Arizona desert. He had trailed Wallace patiently, doggedly, like an Indian; he would get him in another two or three days.

He came out of the desert late that afternoon and into a green belt of cottonwood trees to the little settlement nestling among them. More than twelve years had passed since the Apache raid on the place, but it had changed little during the passing of time. Just a line of adobe buildings along one side of the "street" for a distance of three hundred feet. There were cabins and little plots of tilled land scattered around, the population not more than fifty or seventy-five.

This included the floating prospectors, bearded and cantankerous old fellows who were unafraid of the Apaches, bands of Mexican robbers, or the very devil himself; the men wanted by peace officers; the pack train smugglers from below the border; and now and then the groups of hard-eyed hunters who made a business of raiding small groups of Apache women and children and carrying the scalps down into Sonora and Chihuahua to be exchanged for gold Mexican pesos.

These and others preferred to live in a land where life was cheap and often depended upon a fleet horse or a good gun.

This was the place that Cogin rode into that late afternoon, leading a pack horse; a tired-looking, spare-framed man, not at all handsome. He wore a heavy brown mustache, as so many men of the period did. His clothes and gear were dusty, the armpits of the dark shirt wet and salt-encrusted. The cartridge belt around his waist carried .44 caliber shells for the worn gun at his right hip. The second belt over his left shoulder was much heavier because it was weighted down with .45-70 cartridges for the huge single-shot Sharps rifle resting upright in the saddle boot back of his right leg.

A .44 caliber saddle gun might have been all right in cow country, and certainly it would have been more convenient inasmuch as the cartridges were interchangeable for pistol and rifle. But Cogin knew this country better than any in the world, he knew the Apaches and their arms, and he wanted no short-range gun in the event of a running fight.

He had watered his horses in the creek's summer trickle when crossing, and now he rode in under the trees toward the large, circular corral not far away. It was exactly as it had been the morning of the big raid twelve years before when he'd been shot off his horse by a trooper and returned to his family in Kansas. He swung down with the stiff-legged movement of a man many hours in the saddle, and stretched his frame to iron out some of the saddle kinks. From beneath a shed inside the enclosure a man came limping toward him; a small wizened man with a crooked leg. He opened the gate of cottonwood poles, said, "Howdy," and waited as Cogin led his freshly watered mounts inside.

"Any chance to put up my horses for the night?" Cogin asked.

"Be glad to, mister. That's how I make my living. Can't get around much any more."

He stretched out the leg and pulled up his trousers to the knee, displaying a badly scarred shin bone that had been shattered and not properly taken care of. "Got that from an Apache twelve year ago when the red devils pulled a big raid on us here," he exclaimed. "Some fight, thet. Lucky a patrol of soldiers slipped up while they had us cornered. They sure wiped out them red devils. Even caught a white kid who was with 'em. Twelve year ago, that was."

Cogin had pulled up near the shed and was unsaddling. He thought: Yes, I remember the raid, and I remember shooting a leg off a man who was running toward another cabin. I remember that Nino tried to grab me up from the ground when I got shot but couldn't make it.

He said, "I hear they've been pretty busy lately."

The crippled corral man was working at the pack on the other horse. "They hev been. We been stickin' pretty close around here, all except Big Gert. Nothing' ever fazes that woman. One of these days her an' them Mexican packers of hern will wind up over a slow fire, tied head down from a cottonwood limb. That Nino is a mean devil if there ever was one. Slick as a coot. He makes fools outa them soldiers. I'll bet you, mister, that them troopers couldn't catch that Apache if he was within ten feet distant an' they all had lariats."

Cogin didn't reply as he dropped the dangling cinch and reached for the saddle to remove it. His face told nothing. It was blank, expressionless. That was what eleven years among the Apaches had done; sunk in deep.

And now, after all those years, not much had seeped out. He was thinking of Nino, how they had played and fought with each other by turns, and then had become bitter enemies. It made no difference that Nino had tried to grab him off the ground that morning and get him away; they had still been enemies.

He lifted the saddle and carried it beneath the shed and hung it from a peg built into the adobe wall. The sweaty-backed bay ambled off across the circular corral's dung-covered floor to the feed trough, and the pack horse soon followed. Cogin removed the heavy cartridge belt from across his shoulder and hung it from the saddle horn. He removed his hat and wiped at his face; tall, angular, booted and spurred.

"Any place I can get something to eat?" he asked the limping man.

"Last house on the other end of the street. Run by a young Mexican woman. Widder woman whose husband got killed in a fight with some scalp hunter one night in Hornbuckle's place. You don't look like a scalp hunter, mister."

"I'm not," Cogin said.

"Didn't think so. They allus mostly travel in bands. But if you don't mind my saying it, I think you're just plain loco to be riding along through this desert while Nino is cutting and slashing at everything in sight. He'll have you staked out in a flash if he ever catches sight of you. But that's your business and none of mine. You musta had good reasons fer doin' it, and down here we don't ask a man any questions. It ain't healthy sometimes. We tend strictly to our own affairs and expect you to. By the way, they call me Limpy."

Cogin shook and said, "Glad to meet you." He did it perfunctorily and automatically, with no thought of becoming friendly with the man whose leg he'd almost shot off that day in the long ago. He was thinking of Nino.

I've always known he'd become a chief some day, he thought. He had what it takes for leadership: brains and daring and a blind hatred for the White Eyes who had killed his mother and brother.

He had been that kind of a youth, and cruel even beyond Apache standards. At sixteen he had helped a bunch of bucks work on a captured soldier. Cogin could still remember how the unconscious man, tied to a post and mutilated an inch at a time for three days running, had been scalped alive; how Nino had picked up a live coal and dropped it into the bloody place where the knife had cut.

Strangely enough, he had felt envy of Nino for thinking up such a wonderful thing to do to the hated White Eyes trooper. For at sixteen, after eleven years with them, he had known no other life, had taken it all for granted, and did not consider torture to be cruel.

And now Nino was the deadliest of their slashing raiders. He was keeping the soldiers busy while the rest of the various bands hunted high in the mountain country to lay in a supply of winter food.

Cogin turned toward the corral gate and looked through the poles to the open doorways of the line of small, low adobe buildings. Here and there he saw men lounging in the shade that was now out in the street; quiet-talking men seemingly without a care in the world. They might be smugglers, fugitives from the law, scalp hunters or one of a dozen other things. His mind classified them automatically while it turned from thoughts of Nino and the raid that day in the long ago when he had tried to kill the limping man back there in the corral. He was thinking of Wallace now, wondering if the man was still here or had gone on.

Wallace either had heard that Cogin was after him or he had suspected it, for the man had fled steadily, just as doggedly as Cogin had followed him; never stopping more than two days in a place, always from a day to a week ahead. Traveling fast and light and with plenty of money from two banks he had held up before committing the terrible crime of assault and the murder of a young girl, Cogin's sister.

Cogin was eyeing the street again. He turned to the man Limpy. "Been any strangers come through during the past two or three days?"

The man Limpy gave him a stare that was almost beady-eyed. It was chilly. "No savvy, mister."

"The rest of these horses belong to men you know?"

Again that unwavering, beady-eyed look. "I wouldn't know, friend."

Cogin unsnapped the leather strap lying tight across the top of the gun sheath to keep the weapon from jolting out while riding. He snapped it out of the way on the back side of the sheath against his leg and loosed the worn weapon in the shiny leather. He opened the corral gate, closed it behind him, and moved toward the row of adobes fifty yards distant. Doors and windows were open, and in the sand two half grown pups romped and growled and bit at each other playfully. He was aware that the few loungers sitting in chairs were watching him without appearing to do so; curious yet with almost complete indifference unless they themselves were being trailed.

Cogin moved through the hard-packed sand, glancing in through the open doorways at rooms which were sparsely furnished with beds and tarps on dirt floors amid the usual litter of riding gear piled helter-skelter to be found where womenless men live. He nodded to a man here and there with curt courtesy but did not speak. There was a small saloon about midway along the line of adobes, and Cogin went inside into coolness and up to a crude bar some six or seven feet in length.

He didn't want a drink because he had never learned to acquire a taste for the white man's whiskey and beer. He had learned to drink *tiswin*, the strong corn beer that was the favorite drink of the Apaches, and now for a period of more than twelve years he had drunk hardly at all.

There were no customers present, just an aged Mexican sweeping the hard-packed dirt floor back of the bar. He served up a drink, and Cogin paid for it and then tossed it off. Not much chance of information here. He could wait until later. Right now the drink was warming his insides and taking away saddle fatigue and sharpening up his appetite. Cogin moved out into the open again, the wariness upon him as it had been in every town he had come through during the past months. Wallace was travelling fast, fleeing the law and, should be aware of Cogin's pursuit, the man following him grimly.

There was a small store run by an old Chinese, but it too was deserted. It and the saloon back there, plus the corral, appeared to be the only business establishments in the unnamed settlement. Cogin saw the smoke wisping up from a dozen cabins and speculated that if Wallace was still here he might be holed up with one of the men in the latter's adobe.

He forgot Wallace and went on toward the house of the Mexican woman, his eyes seeing everything that was within vision. That was what eleven years among the Apaches had done; he had been schooled in such things at the expert hands of the older warriors when he was a child.

He cared nothing about women, even the young sister who was now dead and who had never quite gotten over her awe of him. Nino hadn't cried when the scalp hunters had surprised and killed the small band of women and children, among which was his mother, and there had been no emotion in Cogin's face when he learned of his own family tragedy. He had merely picked out the two best horses on his father's big ranch not far from Abilene, Kansas, and come after the man. There had been no good-bye either to his family or the men on the ranch, for he had never made friends with any man. They knew him only as a silent man who liked to be alone, who seldom spoke, who would kill at the drop of a hat. A man with fathomless blue eyes that never changed expression.

Cogin stepped into the room through the open doorway.

Chapter 2

IT WAS about twelve or thirteen feet square, with a hard-packed dirt floor, and contained only a table large enough to seat four or five men on each side. There were a few chairs, presumably for those who had to wait their turn at the table. Four or five men were eating as Cogin entered. Through a doorway leading into the kitchen he saw two young urchins playing on the dirt floor and a buxom young Mexican woman bent over the stove, her hand busy with a stirring spoon. This was the widow of the dead Mexican smuggler, killed in a fight with one of the scalp hunters.

A luscious woman who, in a place where the population was preponderantly male, would not be long without another man.

He said in Spanish, *"Tiene usted algun cena para me, señora?"* Have you some supper for me, lady?

"Si, señor." She nodded toward the table. *"Sedentee."* Sit down.

She nodded again, this time toward the back door, and told him in Spanish that if he wanted to wash up there was basin and towel outside. He stepped past the two urchins, poured water into a clay bowl on a bench, and washed the stains of travel from his face. The towel had done similar service for many other men since being washed, and he smelled the sweat and dirt in it as he dried his face and rubbed at the stubble of whiskers. He would have to heat some water and shave after supper.

Birds were trilling among the cottonwoods' green foliage, a final salute and tribute to another wonderful day.

They fluttered and shrieked and fought mock battles among the leaves, and kept wary eyes out for the big hawks that had a habit of smashing down out of nowhere to pick up a final meal of the evening. Out by a small lot a cow, her udder heavy with milk, chewed on her cud and waited patiently for the woman to come out and turn her in to where the hungry calf bawled impatiently for its supper. Cogin returned to the front room.

One of the men was saying, "You can never tell about them red devils. That's what we thought twelve years ago when they hit us that morning. Not a sign of anything anywhere. It was just as nice and quiet as could be. I'd got up at daybreak and opened up my saloon like I always do. Limpy—his name wasn't Limpy then—he was leadin' a horse down to the creek to water it. Then they hit us like a streak of lightning. I heard Limpy yell as they shot a leg out from under him, and then we covered him with rifle fire until he could crawl into his cabin and get the door barred. We drove 'em off three times during the next two hours. They'd run by a corral and shoot down a horse or anything else in sight; just anything at all to kill something, no matter what. They set fire to some of the pole corrals but didn't have any luck with the cabins on account of them being adobe. We were still going at it hot and heavy when that patrol of troopers broke in at a run and caught 'em flat-footed. They killed eight of them and wounded another before the red devils could spur away."

Cogin seated himself beside the speaker, a small, wiry-looking, bright-eyed man of possibly fifty. The man turned to look at him and said, "Howdy, stranger. I'm Hornbuckle. Got the only bar in town, a small one a few doors up the street. First drink is always on the house."

"Thanks, I've already had it," Cogin said.

He saw the questioning looks the men cast at each other as he spoke, just as a hundred other times in the past men had looked at each other upon hearing his strange accent.

It had been difficult, at sixteen, to learn a new language

from the white woman who said that she was his mother and that he had been stolen by the Apaches out in Arizona Territory when he was five. He had been unmoved at her story of how they had finally despaired of ever getting him back and had returned to Kansas. He felt no affection for her, no affection for any human being on earth. He was a man alone, without fear, without emotion. There was no particular anger in his heart for the savage, vicious man whose trail he had followed so patiently and doggedly for hundreds of miles. He would merely keep on it until he caught up with the man and shot him. If he could surprise the man in camp, he'd bury him to the neck in an ant hill and sit there and watch him die.

It was as simple as that.

One of the men said, "I heard about that fight, Horn. Seems like they had some white men with 'em that got wounded and was captured."

Hornbuckle nodded again, and now Cogin remembered him. Hornbuckle had stood over him with the soldiers that morning when they had been about to dispatch him until a sergeant had noticed Cogin's blue eyes.

"That's right," Hornbuckle nodded. "He was shot right through a shoulder and lying there on the ground bleeding, but not letting out a peep. He just laid there and glared back at us. Wouldn't even talk with the Apache scouts working for the soldiers. And when they took him to the fort to the hospital till his folks could come after him, they had to keep him chained to his bed."

"I'd like to have got a crack at him," grunted a very heavy-set, seedy-looking rider, busy gorging himself with food. "They wouldn'ta needed any chains then, I can tell you."

Hornbuckle turned to Cogin. "Just get in?" he asked.

Cogin nodded.

"We don't ask any questions of any man who comes in here. Their business is their own. So is ourn."

"If you mean how long am I staying, I'll be moving on in the morning, most likely."

"No questions intended. Just thought I'd let you know."

"I'm not a law officer, if that's what you mean. So I won't be asking many."

Nor did he intend to, except to find out if Wallace had come through recently. He knew that the man had been through, the tracks of the man's horse having told him that; for Cogin could trail and read sign as few white men could, the result of his early life among the Apaches. It was a question of whether the man was still in the settlement or how long it had been since his departure.

The man sitting opposite Cogin was obviously a cheap tinhorn gambler down on his luck. His white shirt was soiled almost beyond recognition, open at the neck. There was no string tie supporting a diamond or two, no rings on his fingers. He had the face of a cadaver, the stringiest neck and largest Adam's apple Cogin had ever seen. With each swallow the bulge rolled up and down and gave the man the appearance of just having swallowed whole a hard-boiled egg.

"Like you, stranger, my name don't matter," he said to Cogin. "You just call me One-Card. We usually have a small game in Horn's place nights," he added suggestively.

"Sorry, I've never played cards," Cogin said curtly, and again saw the furtive, questioning looks in their eyes as they heard his strange accent.

He was one of them in that he was booted, spurred, gun-belted; obviously a man who knew cattle. But that accent . . . Probably some furriner, they thought.

The heavy-set puncher sat next to the gambler; obviously some kind of a loafer because his fat stomach protruded almost obscenely over the top of his belt. He was shoveling down food in great gulps as though into a bottomless pit, his gluttony sickening to see. His eyes had strayed through the doorway into the kitchen more than once, and Cogin thought he understood what was on the man's mind. Plenty of food at all times, plus a woman.

"I'm Bartlett, but they just call me Bart fer short," he volunteered, wiping at his mouth with a shirt sleeve. "Do a little hoss tradin' with some of the boys who come through in a hurry and ain't too pertickler," he added, winking suggestively like some grinning gargoyle.

The fourth man said nothing, finishing off a final cup of coffee.

The Mexican woman came in with a platter of steaming food in her hands and smilingly placed it in front of Cogin. He fell to eating in customary silence, listening idly to the desultory conversation. From out in the street he heard the sound of loping hoofs, and then they stopped just outside of the doorway. There was the sound of a boot hitting the ground, the rattle of a spur rowel. Then a woman's voice called out, "Hello, Limpy, you little sawed-off runt. How's tricks?"

Chapter 3

COGIN LOOKED up from his food as she stepped into the doorway, the man limpy behind her; and in many ways she was a remarkable specimen of womanhood. She wore a black hat, broad of brim, and with a needle-pointed crown that made her appear much taller than her natural height of about five feet nine inches. Her blue man's shirt was open at the strong-looking throat, revealing an expanse of browned skin above her firm-looking, ample bosom. She was booted, spurred, leather-skirted, and a quirt dangled from a thong around her right wrist. At her right hip, below a cartridge belt, lay a sheathed pistol.

Cogin guessed her age as about thirty-three and her weight at one hundred and fifty-five pounds. She looked as strong and capable as any man in the place.

"Well," she greeted him boisterously, "looks like the joint is jammed full."

"You can have my place, Gert," Hornbuckle said, rising to his feet. "I'm finished."

She tossed her hat into a corner, followed it with the quirt, and swung a leg over the stool, seating herself beside Cogin as Limpy followed her in. Hornbuckle lit his pipe and leaned against the wall that separated kitchen from the "dining room." The silent fourth man got up and was replaced by the corral man Cogin had crippled in the raid that day twelve years before. Cogin ate in silence.

"Anything new about the 'Paches?" the woman asked of nobody in particular.

"Fellow came through here yesterday and got a fresh hoss," Bart, the big-bellied eater, still stuffing himself, replied. "They hit a ranch about sixty miles north of here and then lit a shuck. Didn't do much damage. Soldiers are out after 'em, but you know about how much chance they'll have ketchin' them slippery devils. None. None a-tall. It just ain't safe to be travelin' alone around this country any more."

"Oh, I dunno," replied Hornbuckle, puffing. "Some men don't seem to think so . . . like the stranger here. Neither did Wallace."

Wallace! So he's been here and left, Cogin thought. I wonder how long since. Maybe I can find out later.

"How's business, Gert?" asked the gambler, One-Card.

"Oh, so-so," shrugged the woman. "My Mexican packers came in with three loads today. One thing you can say for those boys: they're as tough and fearless as they come, Apaches or no 'Paches."

"They won't be if Nino happens to run across 'em," put in Hornbuckle, and added to no one in particular, probably for Cogin's benefit, "She makes more money than all the rest of us put together."

"Pah!" retorted the woman good-naturedly. "Smuggling mescal and tequila? It's a dog's life. Them tightwad sallonmen in the mining camps would skin a poor woman to the teeth if I didn't lean over their bars and curse the stuffings out of them. I just get by and that's all."

"I'll bet!" laughed Hornbuckle.

"It's the truth. Just about the time I get some money ahead and figure I can get out of here and into something where there's real money, I lose a pack train to Mexican bandits or don't get paid when some saloon goes broke. I'm in the same boat as the rest of you starving fellows. For two cents I'd give up the whole business and go back to dealing in one of the gambling halls."

"Why don't you finance me in a small place, Gert?" the seedy tinhorn suggested. "It wouldn't take much, and I can skin those suckers fast and make both of us some money."

The woman's frank eyes looked into those of the man sitting across the narrow table, and a snort of contempt came from her. "You think I'd back up a cheap tinhorn like you with my hard-earned money? If you can skin suckers, what are you doing down here?"

"Perhaps I have no choice in the matter, Gert?"

"Jail bait for some officer, eh? You hang out down here along the creek and mooch drinks and try to win a few dollars now and then. And you want *me* to set you up in business. Listen, One-Card. Any time I open up my own joint I'll either deal at one of the games myself or supervise it. And I wouldn't even give you a job as a swamper."

"Think you might get out one of these days, Gert?" asked Hornbuckle.

"You bet I'm getting out!" the woman replied emphatically, removing her gloves and tucking them inside the circle of the cartridge belt. "You think I'm going to spend the rest of my life down here living like a man, smuggling stinking Mexican liquor to the swill houses and letting them take the big profits? I need just one good stake and then I'll be back where I belong: In a low-cut dress back of a gaming table, taking the suckers for their money."

"Then," the quietly smoking Hornbuckle replied,

"don't make the mistake that I did, Gert. Get out while you're young and have some drive left. That's what I was going to do years ago when I slipped into this country to lie low for a while until things cooled down. Figured to stay here just long enough for the law to forget and to build myself up enough of a stake to start in new some place else. Every year that's what I figured. 'Next year,' I'd say. 'Next year I'll pull out and make the plunge.' Well, next year didn't ever come, and one day I woke up to the fact that I'd waited too long to pull up roots and go replant somewhere else. So here I sit in this godforsaken hole, selling raw liquor at ten cents a shot and usually not too many customers. I sold two dollars and eighty cents' worth yesterday. Twenty-eight drinks from six yesterday morning until eleven last night. I've been here too long, and the only thing that can take me out is a quick stake that I haven't got and most likely won't ever have."

"Well, I haven't," grunted back the woman beside Cogin. He was aware that she was attractive in a hard sort of way, and he could smell her faint and attractive perfume, though it elicited no response in him. There had never been any room in his life, in his thoughts, for a woman. "All I need is a stake and I'll be hauling my freight out of here *muy pronto* for greener pastures. Tell you what, Horn: when we make it let's put up a big joint together, you and I. You can handle the bar end, and I'll handle the dance hall girls as dealers. Nothing but women dealers trained by me." She twisted on the hard stool to look at him. "I'm dead serious, Horn. Give me a good bunch of keen girls to train and I'll trim those suckers within five minutes after they hit the place. Just all women dealers in low-cut gowns; no men."

"I suppose it could be done, all right," he admitted, and went on smoking thoughtfully.

She turned back, and her penetrating gaze rested on Cogin's face. He was aware of it but paid her no heed.

"Which direction did you come from?" she asked bluntly.

He said, "North," and went on eating, without looking at her.

"Packing a badge?"

Bart guffawed loudly and looked at Cogin. "You know what she means by that, stranger? Her husband died sorta sudden like, that's what."

The woman looked over at him, her eyes chilly. "Don't you ever again make a remark like that, Bart, or I'll crack your head open. How my husband died or why I'm down here is none of your business. The quicker you get that through your thick skull the better off you'll be."

"I'm not packing a badge," Cogin replied.

"Good. Then you're welcome here. Hey!" she shouted in through the doorway to the Mexican woman. "Bring me some grub. I'm going to fill up and then beat the pants off any man who wants to play poker. And that includes you, One-Card, if you've got any money—which you undoubtedly have not."

"Maybe the stranger here, who doesn't play cards, will stake me," suggested the gambler.

"Not interested," Cogin answered curtly, and went on with his meal.

"Has he told you his name, Horn?" asked the woman over her shoulder.

"We haven't asked, Gert," Hornbuckle replied.

Cogin rose from the table, stepped to the kitchen doorway, asked the price of the meal, and paid in small silver coins. The Mexican woman bobbed her dark head and smiled and said, *"Gracias, señor. Muchas gracias."* Cogin rolled a cigarette and looked at Hornbuckle.

"Mind if I ask you a couple of questions in private?"

The wiry little saloonman looked him over, and into his eyes came the same kind of wary chill that had been present in the eyes of the man Limpy, now waiting for his meal.

"Nothing private around here, mister," he answered with just a touch of brittleness in his voice. "We're all friends here, sort of all one of a kind. What's on your mind?"

"Been any strangers in here the last couple or three days? One man in particular, playing it solo."

"You just came in," was the pointed reply.

"About thirty-seven years old. Knife scar over his left cheek bone. Brown, drooping mustache with sharp points. Square built. Packs two guns sometimes."

Every eye in the little room was on him now, the woman's very hard and penetrating as though she were trying to probe back of his lean features to see what lay in his mind. She said, "What did he do? Maybe he wasn't here."

"I trailed him here," Cogin said. "He was here within the past three days, I'm pretty certain."

"You talk plenty funny," she told him. "I've seen a lot of furriners in the places I used to work in. Got to where I could tell what country they came from by their accent. But that one of yourn has me baffled. Never heard it before. What did he do?" she repeated.

"Wallace? He's killed nineteen men and held up a few banks . . . among other things."

"Hmmm," she said thoughtfully, mostly to herself. "I knew he was running from something. He had to be to keep on hitting out through this desert filled with 'Paches. He was here, sure. Camped at my place down the creek a ways for two days while he rested up his horses. Played poker in Horn's with us nights. And you're after him and you ain't packin' a badge."

"No badge."

She twisted around to look at Hornbuckle, a slight frown creasing her rather attractive face. No doubt about it, she had at one time been a strikingly beautiful woman. Cogin thought vaguely and disinterestedly that, had she not worked in dance halls at the gaming tables, she would have made some hard-working rancher an ideal wife.

She said, "If he's not packing a badge, Horn, what other reason would he have for trailing Wallace?"

Hornbuckle looked at her speculatively and didn't reply for a moment. He finally removed the wet stem of the corncob pipe from his mouth.

"Maybe for personal reasons."

She shook her blonde head. The hair was piled high in long braids like those of a silken rope. "Possibly, but I don't think so. He said Wallace had robbed banks, and I know that's true, for I saw some of the big wads of money he always kept near a gun at night. That means a reward for him. A bounty. Our friend with the strange accent is a bounty hunter, Horn. What about it, mister?"

"Just tell me when he came in, when he left, and in which direction," Cogin said impatiently.

"Oh, like that, eh?" she snapped at him.

"Never mind, lady. It really don't matter a lot. I can pick up his tracks in the morning."

"Of course you can," she half jeered at him. "You said you trailed him this far, didn't you? You come in here with a face like a canyon boulder and a strange kind of voice I never heard before. You ain't no ordinary cowpuncher or horse thief. You don't pack a badge and you ain't the kind who gives a damn about anybody or anything except maybe money. So I've got you pegged. *You're a bounty hunter, out for scalp money.* Well, you won't find out anything else in here, so don't ask any more questions."

He was unaware that something about him, his aloofness and indifference, had aroused strange stirrings within her; that she lived her life alone and manless in the settlement because it was her code, a throwback to her dance hall days when a girl, even a dealer, had to have her guard up all the time. She had never revealed what had actually caused the death of her late husband, leaving the men who knew her to guess. And now this stranger had come along, indifferent to the fact that she was an attractive woman in a womanless place, and the thought stung her just a bit.

Cogin stepped to the doorway and tossed away the butt of the cigarette. "Believe whatever you wish," he said curtly to her and, for that matter, to the others. "Just as long as I know that he was here recently, I'll get him."

"The devil you will!" came her jeering voice, stinging at him as he had stung her by his cold indifference.

He went on out into the evening shade again, striding back toward the corral to unpack his bedroll and get at his razor. In the room there was silence for a few moments, and then the woman got to her feet, all thought of food temporarily forgotten.

"I've got him pegged, all right, Horn," she insisted. "I'm positive. That icy-faced gent is a money hunter."

"Maybe not," he said dubiously.

"What happens when a man sticks up a bank?" she demanded. "Does the banker get on his horse and go after him when the sheriff fails? Not on your life. He puts out a reward and lets the other fellow do the riding and dirty work. This is strictly a reward job. I'd bet on it."

"How come you're so positive, Gert?" asked the saloon-man.

"Listen, Horn," she said earnestly. "I held out on you boys. I told you Wallace had quite some money, but I didn't say how much. Well, it was plenty! In two canvas bags, all paper gold-backs. I didn't want to say anything because I saw a chance for a quick stake to get out of here and get back to civilization, to do the kind of work I'm best fitted to do. Wallace didn't tell me where he got the money and I didn't ask. I wasn't interested just as long as he *had* it. I tried to get him to pull out of here with me and go some place and open up a gambling hall. He wanted to do it, too, except that he had to get across that Mexican border for a few months and lay low till things cooled down. That much he told me. He promised he'd come back in a few months and we'd make it. I was all resigned to a period of waiting. And now this fellow who talks so strange comes in on his trail. And I can tell you right now, Horn, that with this icy-faced gent after him, Wallace is not coming back! So where does that leave Big Gert again? Right behind the deuce."

"Tough luck," commented Hornbuckle.

"Tough luck?" she cried out. "The one chance I've had in four years to get back on top, and now it's blown to pieces by this man who just left. Horn, I want that money plus what he's probably got on his head in rewards. I'm going after it."

"How? Where?"

"Wallace was heading for Chihauhua City. That much he told me when he left. I asked him why he hadn't gone straight to El Paso and taken the stage down, but he said he couldn't risk it. There was a man on his trail he had to shake off first. That's why he cut a circle way over in this country."

"And you think you could overtake him?"

"Easy. It's not too far to the border now, and he'll feel safe once he gets across. He only left day before yesterday, as you know. My packers met him on the way up. There's been no wind to cover his horses' tracks, and trailing will be easy. We can wait until that bird with the strange voice gets to sleep and pull out of here tonight on some good horses. We'll be miles ahead by tomorrow. And if that bounty hunter tries to overhaul us, a few good rifle slugs will change his mind. What do you say, Horn—you and me, the stake we've been looking for?"

Three stools scraped on the hard-packed dirt floor almost simultaneously. The man Limpy, the heavy-set, gluttonous Bart, the seedy-looking gambler called One-Card. His monstrosity of an Adam's apple rolled up and then down his thin throat as he looked at the two other men at the table.

He said to the woman, "Why you and Horn, Gert? By what right just you two? I thought it kind of funny you let him cotton up to you when you're allus so stand-offish toward all men. I should have remembered that you once was a dance hall clipper. You can count us in on the deal."

"You can count yourselves right out on the deal too."

One-Card shook his head. "We're either in or we go straight to that stranger right now and spill the whole works. You and Horn ain't the only ones who'd like to get out of this hole and make a fresh start. And besides, if there is trouble from him you may need some help and lots of it. That gent is dangerous."

"That just about says it all, Gert," the man Bart put in. "Better take a smaller cut and play it safer. You and Horn wouldn't be no match for a man like him. That boy is as tough as they come, and you oughta have sense enough to know it and not let your greed cause you to do somethin' foolish."

"I'm crippled up from an Apache bullet, but I can still ride and shoot," Limpy put in quietly. "Count us in, Gert, or we spill the whole works. With the money from them banks, plus the rewards this feller is after, there'll be enough for a stake for all of us."

She looked from one face to another, back to Hornbuckle, still smoking thoughtfully, then without a word sat down and began to eat the food the Mexican woman placed before her.

Chapter 4

DARK CAME down softly that evening, moving in cool silence except for the birds that now chattered not loudly but with occasional sleepy chirps. A few lights pinpointed the coolness that had come first among the trees and then begun spreading up the gentle slopes of the desert. All day long it had been burning hot out there while the rattlesnakes coiled themselves in the shade of cacti and the field mice remained underground and the big night owls remained asleep in their homes in hollow cottonwood trunks.

From the open doorway of Hornbuckle's small saloon with its short bar of rough planking came the sound of much laughter, sometimes a little high-pitched and off key, and the click of poker chips. There was a penny ante game going while four men and a woman waited for the night to advance.

Fifty yards from the back of the corral Cogin had spread out his tarp bedroll beneath a big cottonwood and lain down to rest a bit; to smoke and to think. Now he rose, took his shaving outfit, and went toward the home of the Mexican woman. He passed the open door of Hornbuckle's and saw the game in progress, a few idle loungers, and passed on.

She was coming back from the corral, carrying a pail of milk and followed by the two fatherless urchins, tagged by a mewing kitten and a nondescript pup, all milk-hungry.

"Water for the shaving?" she asked. "Of course, *señor*. One moment and I will have it for you."

She brought the water from the kitchen stove and gave him a clean towel. She stood idly in the doorway and watched as he scraped away a three days' growth of pig bristle from his cheeks and chin.

"You have come a long way, I think, *señor*," she said.

"Yes, a very long way."

"And you have far to go?"

"A bit further, I think. To Mexico."

"My home was in Mexico, *señor*. I came here with my husband. He is buried out there behind the corral."

He was sloshing water over his clean-shaven face, washing away the suds. He turned, towel in hand. "Then why do you not return?"

She shrugged as only a Mexican woman can shrug. "I have the two children and no money, *señor*."

There it was again, he thought. Another lost one in this unnamed settlement, not a resident but a prisoner in the desert, without the one key that could free her: money. They were all the same. All except Wallace. It was ironical that Wallace the murderer had, through the use of his guns and a display of daring and recklessness, brought the key with him. A key consisting of two canvas bags filled with gold-back notes taken at gun point and at the cost of two dead cashiers and one wounded constable left behind.

Cogin finished and left her, returning along the street where the laughter still came from Hornbuckle's place and the few loungers sat with chairs tipped back against the walls of their dirty, gear-infested adobe abodes. He returned to his bedroll, removed his boots, and lay there on his back, looking up at the branches of the tree where the birds chirped sleepily; looking at the sky beyond.

He saw the twinkling of the stars and remembered the many legends the Apaches had taught him of the spirits up there. Once one of them cut a long flaming path in a downward curve and then went out. One moment it was a bright constellation; the next, a cooling dark mass speeding on through space to the end of time, unto eternity.

There was a half framed thought in his mind not to go back after he had caught and killed Wallace. He felt strangely like that falling star up there; engaged in motion but without emotion, going on aimlessly because certain laws, not man-made, seemed to make it impossilbe for the star to turn around and go back.

There was nothing for him back in Kansas on the big ranch of his father. No friendship, no affection, no ties that impregnated in him a desire to return. He had lived too long among the Apaches to adjust himself fully to the life of his family in Kansas. He had remained too long among the whites to return to the Apaches. . . .

"Hey, what in the blazes have we got here?" a voice suddenly demanded, and he opened his eyes there near the corral and looked up into the faces of the men standing around him.

Hornbuckle was there, much younger now, and carried a rifle in one hand. With him were some White Eyes soldiers; three of them. Thirty or forty others were walking around among the sprawled bodies scattered over an area of one hundred yards; for the raiders had been so absorbed in their attack that the one from behind had come as a complete surprise.

"He's only a kid but he's a mean-looking little devil," Hornbuckle said.

"Go get the lieutenant," a sergeant ordered a corporal.

"Lieutenant hell! Give me one shot from this pistol through his head and we won't need no lieutenant. We ain't packing in any wounded 'Paches."

"I said go get the lieutenant! Take a look at them eyes. They're blue, and he's lighter-skinned than the others. He's white. Go get Lieutenant Egglestrom!"

The blood was still running a bit from the gaping would in his shoulder, high up, proving the shocking power of a Sharps .45-70 rifle. The big bullet had somersaulted him out of the saddle, and Nino had done his best, which wasn't enough. He had flashed by on his pony and swooped down and grabbed for one of Cogin's hands, but his hold had slipped and Nino had kept right on at a full run while the soldiers cursed and tried to reload their rifles for more shots.

He had lain there and eyed them with a tight mouth and coldly burning eyes and waited for them to kill him, for he couldn't understand a word of their garbled White Eyes tongue.

This White Eyes officer who came was slim and ramrod straight and still carried a saber in one hand. He had been dispatching a couple of the wounded warriors who were unable to crawl away.

The officer shouted something and waved, and one of the Apache scouts who had helped to tail and surprise the raiders came running. He was a middle-aged warrior that Cogin knew well, Tanaca, and he spoke the garbled tongue of these White Eyes. The officer talked and pointed down, and the scout nodded and grinned. He looked at Cogin, on his back on the ground, naked from the waist up.

"He says that you have the light skin and the eyes of one of them, that you are not an Apache."

"He speaks with a forked tongue like all White Eyes. I am an Apache."

More talk, more garbled words, and then the middle-aged warrior who now worked for the soldiers grinned again and spoke to him once more.

"He speaks with a straight tongue, Poco. I know this thing to be true, because eleven grasses ago I was on the raid when you were taken from the ranch. I helped your father carry you off, and now you will not return to him from this raid. The White Eyes officer say that you will be taken to their camp. When you are well you will be sent far away to the people we took you from."

"I am not a White Eyes. I'm an Apache!"

"You are a White Eyes. . . ."

The hospital room at the fort was of adobe, plastered smooth inside and whitewashed, and he found himself in a bed of the kind the White Eyes slept in. It was a foolish kind of contraption and not comfortable as his bed of deerskins spread on the ground inside the *jacal* of his father. He lay there covered with bandages around the shoulders and neck and watched the nurse with burning eyes.

Her nose was too thin, not broad and dark like the beautiful Apache girls. Her eyes were the hated blue of his own, the color of which always had shamed him, and for that reason alone he would have killed her had the opportunity presented itself. She was one of those useless White Eyes women whose back and shoulders were not strong enough to carry a baby lashed to it and a deerskin sack full of berries on top of her head. He simply couldn't understand why her young officer husband was so proud of her and why the other officers so envied the man because of his beautiful young wife.

He turned his young back on her as she smiled a goodnight and blew out the lamp, and an hour later one of the sentries found him crawling along the ground of the compound, dragging himself with his one good arm. After that they manacled him by one wrist to the bed and the Apache interpreter told him that in a few weeks his White Eyes mother and father would arrive to take him away.
. . .

The whitewashed walls of the room faded out and darkness came again and Cogin shifted his body on the tarp bedroll. Presently he dropped off to sleep.

He slept the sleep of the tired and healthy, though sometime during the night he thought vaguely that he heard in his sleep the sound horses make while walking slowly through soft sand. He did not awaken sufficiently to investigate but slept through until daybreak. He lay there for a few moments in the grey dawn, his face and body drinking in the coolness of early morning before the sun would soon drive it away, yawning and stretching the lethargy from his now rested body. Finally he sat up, rolled a cigarette, pulled on his boots, and went toward the creek to wash his face in the cool waters.

Presently he returned and picked up the tarp bedroll and carried it over to the shed in the corral. The man Limpy wasn't around, and Cogin guessed that the poker game had not broken up until late and that the man was still asleep. That was what happened to a man when he settled down too long in one place. As Hornbuckle had so judiciously pointed out the evening before, you got into a rut of routine too comfortable to climb out of, the bloom of energy and ambition faded, and you gradually went to seed.

Cogin watered his own horses, found feed and set them to eating, got curry comb and brush from his pack. The sweaty backs of his two mounts had long since dried from rolls in powdered horse dung, a few good shakes, and exposure to the cool night air. He worked away at their backs until they were smooth and sleek. He wanted no galled horses to slow him up on the trail that must end only in the death of Wallace. These were the pick of the big ranch up in Kansas and he took good care of them.

The settlement was dead, devoid of all life and movement, as he went down to the house of the Mexican woman to have his breakfast.

Chapter 5

THE DESERT is supposed to be a dry, barren land of brush and cacti and rocks and eroded gullies and arroyos, cut and slashed by the flash floods during the rainy season; a land of long, burning stretches of dry waste country devoid of all human life. But on this particular day had a crow flapped up out of the cottonwoods by the little settlement and flown a straight line almost due south toward the Mexican border forty miles away, it would have been found to be not so.

The crow would have seen a lone rider leading a pack horse and following almost leisurely the tracks made by the horses of four men and one determined woman. It would have seen those five, miles further on, first spread out and then finally converge on the tracks made by the two horses of a man named Wallace. The crow would have seen a tired, dusty troop of cavalrymen coming out of the wastes after another futile patrol in search of the elusive Nino, currently the most hard-raiding of the various bands of those fierce-visaged warriors.

Had the crow flown on far enough south and into Mexico, gone deep toward the Sierra Madre—the Mother Mountain—it would have seen the murderer Bas Wallace holed up comfortably at a small spring, plenty of food in his pack, though with fear in his heart. He had met Cogin on their ranch up in Kansas, knew the man's Apache background, knew what to expect. As a gun fighter with nineteen men to his credit, he had no fear of the grim rider he knew was on his trail. He would have turned at bay and killed him; stopped in any town, waited, and shot him down. But Cogin wouldn't come into a town in the open the way a "white man" would, and that was why Wallace the murderer still fled.

And the crow would have seen Victorio Lopez, a self-styled young bandit leader, and his men camped deep in the wilderness of the wild Sierra Madre.

But Cogin saw none of these things as he followed the tracks southward on that warm, clear morning. The tracks told him that the five money-mad riders had traveled fast during the night, driving two pack horses ahead of them. There was urgency in the tracks, the way the toe marks dug in as they had galloped and trotted by turn.

Cogin himself was in no hurry. He knew he could overhaul them. He himself knew a little about night riding.

He let his two horses set a good pace, knowing from years down here with the Apaches just how fast to travel. He rode until just before noon and finally pulled up in the shade of a giant sahuaro that grew on the lip of a washed out arroyo. The cactus and the bank afforded shade for the horses and for himself. He poured water from his wet canvas sacks into nose bags, let them drink and then fed them lightly from some grain carried by the pack horse. There wasn't much water left when he finished, but this worried him little; for he knew every waterhole in all this dry, desolate land as well as his father up in Kansas knew his grazing ranges.

For three hours he rested the horses and himself while the sun swung overhead and then pushed over the west. The heat had not lessened when he changed his saddle to the pack horse, switched the pack to the horse he had ridden all morning, and again took up the trail. He traveled steadily for most of the afternoon, stopping at a waterhole hidden in a rocky gully to replenish his supply of the precious liquid. Half an hour later when he topped a ridge he saw the soldiers.

There were about thirty of them, he judged, led by a young lieutenant and accompanied by two Apache scouts. One of them Cogin recognized at a glance—Tanaca, a man much older now. He was the middle-aged man who had been present the morning of the raid on the settlement when Cogin's life as an Apache had ended and his new life as a White Eyes began.

The scouts were apparently guiding the troop to the waterhole, and Cogin pulled up and waited. They rode up, tired and dusty, the blue of their uniforms almost white from the alkaline, powdery dust. Cogin raised a hand in greeting and the officer replied in kind, riding closer.

"Good afternoon," greeted the officer. He was young, not more than twenty-three, proably not long out of West Point. "I'm Lieutenant Franklin, of the Eighth."

"No sign of Nino, I suppose," Cogin ventured. His eyes had gone to the face of the older of the scouts. He thought: The old devil doesn't look a day older than twelve years ago. And I'll bet my last dollar that he could find Nino if he wanted to badly enough. I guess he's got into a rut too. A twenty-dollar-a-month rut.

Franklin was looking at Cogin with a keen interest tinged with just a bit of resentment. He was young, he was ambitious, and the fact that they had been out for ten days without a sign of Nino irked him. Cogin thought, seeing what lay in the man's eyes: You'll feel differently in a few more years, Lieutenant, when you're a slow-moving captain.

"No sign at all," Franklin said curtly. "May I ask where you're headed?"

"I'm trailing five damned fools including a woman," Cogin said dryly. "How far are they ahead?"

"About thirty miles. We met them this morning. I warned them that they should return with us, but they appeared determined to continue. Haven't they sense enough to know that they may end up staked out on the ground? This country is alive with Apaches."

Cogin let that one slide by with a half-smile. He wanted to say: You didn't find any, Lieutenant. Maybe because that grinning old devil there didn't want you to.

He said, "They're pretty hard-case customers, Officer. They can take care of themselves . . . maybe."

"Maybe?" came the half-angry reply. "The military rides the seat out of their pants trying to run down these raiding devils, and for what? To have people go out like that and get themselves killed. And who gets blamed by the people of the Territory? The soldiers, of course."

The older of the scouts had edged his horse forward and was watching Cogin's face closely. Cogin thought: He recognizes me all right. He'd never forget a face even after twelve years.

"Well," said Lieutenant Franklin briskly, "we'd better get forward, men. I suppose it will do no good to urge you to return with us to the safety of civilization."

"None at all, Lieutenant."

"You wouldn't have a chance alone out here, man! Like so many of you civilians of the territory who have never fought the Apaches, you simply fail to realize the danger."

The scout had urged his horse forward a bit closer. Now he grinned that slit-mouthed grin again and spoke. "Long time you go away. No come back. You White Eyes now, Poco."

He was speaking Apache, and a look of astonishment broke over the officer's face as the gutturals came rapidly from Cogin's lips. "Where is Nino?"

"Don't know. Maybe here, maybe long far away."

"You know, Tacana. But he is young and you are old and you can not catch him."

"Catch him some day. You wait."

"I beg your pardon, sir," broke in the astonished officer. "Am I to understand that you speak Apache?"

"Quite fluently, Lieutenant, partly because this old devil here was one of my teachers." And Cogin grinned one of his rare saturnine grins.

He left them, his mind automatically dismissing them as soon as they were behind. He turned to the problem ahead, his one fear that the five up there thirty miles away would come upon Wallace in camp and kill him without warning. That was a job for Cogin to do, and not for the money the man carried. He had simply set out to get the man, and his methodical mind brooked no thought of anybody else doing the job for him.

He rode until dark and then made camp at another spring, which was almost dry. He ate and rested the horses for four hours and then went on through the night, riding until sometime shortly before daybreak. He was far across the Mexican border by now and following the trail deep into Sonora. It was angling eastward toward the state of Chihuahua, strengthening Cogin's belief that Wallace had too much money to hole up in a small place. Chihuahua City was a mecca for every type of American, both fugitive and otherwise; and when a man had gold to pay to certain officials, nothing short of a small army could harm him.

Cogin rode on all that second day, changing horses at regular intervals, the trail still plain ahead. He camped at a small *rancho* that night to rest his tired horses and get them some green feed. The desert had begun to give way to small foothills, and spotted among them were a hundred green patches that told of cultivated fields. By noon that day, when he bought supplies in a tiny village store, the five were only four hours ahead of him. Wallace was a little more than a day ahead, having come through the morning before.

The trail was getting close, and so was the rifle bullet that screamed past Cogin's head just before sundown.

Chapter 6

IT WAS Hornbuckle who had spotted him early that day while the party rested their horses briefly on top of a rocky ridge, for the saloonman was the only one of the party who carried field glasses. He turned in the saddle, lowered the glasses, and in silence returned them to a leather case fastened to the saddle horn.

"Well?" demanded the woman Gert.

"Of course it's him," Hornbuckle grunted. "You should have known it wouldn't be anybody else. He isn't the kind of a man who'd give up just because five of us got the jump on his quarry."

His temper was on edge from the heat, from fatigue, from the alkaline rasp in his throat. The others were much in the same mood. There had been frequent outbursts of temper; men snapping at one another because their nerves were getting raw from the strain and the uncertainty. They were tired of each other's comments, of expressed hopes, of occasional grumbling at the heat and flies and the whole burning country itself. And of course that feeling of distrust of each other was beginning to creep up now that the wanted man was not more than a day or so ahead. This much they had found out by inquiries where Wallace had stopped to water his horses and now and then purchase food and supplies in small villages.

"We've got to stop him," Hornbuckle said finally.

"Of course we've got to stop him," snapped Limpy. "Let's keep going until we find a good place for an ambush, and I'll drop him cold with a rifle. I might be crippled, but I can still shoot."

He used his good leg to gig his horse over to where the two pack horses carrying their supplies were nibbling at a small bush. They moved into motion, and Bart the horse trader spurred up to the fore again to take up his job as tracker. His fat had begun to tell on him now, and the sweat ran down his face in streams and soaked his shirt around the collar. The gambler One-Card rode near Big Gert and stared straight ahead, doubtless daydreaming of the big place he would own and the money he would make after Wallace had been overhauled. Hornbuckle used the glasses more frequently now.

He didn't know whether Cogin had spotted them or

not and doubted it seriously, because the man far back there in the wastes was but a tiny dot through the glasses.

Limpy rode off to one side, herding the two pack horses, the foot to his shot up leg dangling free of the stirrup. The leg had begun to pain him a bit, yet he was the one among the party who had made no complaints. He rode with his small, dark head sunk forward a bit, following the horses automatically but not seeing them. He was unaware of the heat now, standing there in the darkness near the church where she had slipped out to see him a final time, her young face upturned to his.

Sure, I didn't want to do it, honey. But he had no right to keep me from seeing you. He was only your stepfather anyhow, and as mean an old cuss as ever lived. Now look here, Della. I'm skedaddling out of here fast tonight. Where? Out west some place. I'm going to lay low for couple of years in one of them mining camps and make us a big stake . . . sure I can do it, honey. You oughta know I'd do anything for you. But you got to wait a couple of years for me, honey. By then things will be all blown over and I can come back and get you—oh, I know you will. That's what I'm counting on. I'll be back here in a year or two and get you, and we'll go some place and start together like we been planning before that old fool busted things up and I shot his head off. You just wait for me, honey. I'll be back. . . .

He hadn't gone back. He had made one of the copper mining camps all right and gone to work. But when a man is twenty-one with a sixteen-year-old girl waiting for him, impatience sometimes becomes the master of conscience. He had started gambling in the vain hope that he could amass a "stake" in a hurry and return for Della; and when a cheap tinhorn like that one riding beside Gert cleaned him of his savings, a youthful temper and frustration overcame common sense and caution. He had returned to his shack, stuck his pistol in a pocket, gone back and demanded his money. The tinhorn paid with his life for his stubbornness, and the man now known as Limpy paid for his freedom by fleeing into the desert and coming to the settlement.

I'd better build myself a cabin and lay low here for a few months. I can make out somehow until things cool off. Hate to wait another few months before I can go back to Della, but she'll wait. She said she would, and I know she will.

He had built his cabin and settled down to watching the faces of every stranger who came but the law somehow couldn't, or didn't, bother.

Sure, I'll sell you my cabin for twenty dollars, stranger. I'm pulling out next week. Going back to get the prettiest girl that ever lived. Apaches? Naw, them red devils got more sense than to attack this place. No danger here.

Not until the morning two days later when he dragged himself into his cabin with a bullet-shattered leg, knowing that he was crippled for life. Twelve years ago now, and he hadn't gone back because of that twisted shin bone that forced him to walk on this toes because one leg was shorter than the other. He had spent twelve bitter, memory-filled years cursing the Apache who had done it—quite unaware that that same "Apache" was now but a few miles behind, coming on their trail; that he was, unknowingly, going to ambush the very man who had filled Limpy's life with bitterness and frustration.

"Hell, I'll go back!" he said suddenly, unaware that he spoke the words aloud, his head snapping up with a jerk.

He spoke so loud that Big Gert, riding not far away, looked over curiously. "What are you gabbling about, Limpy? The heat got you?"

He ignored the thrust and trotted after the pack horses. It was all clear now. A crippled leg didn't really make any difference when a man had money and a good business such as a livery. And there was always just a chance that Della had never married; that she was back there as he had left her, now about twenty-nine years old.

The afternoon passed swiftly for him now as the party

drove deeper into the desert. They could see the mountains far, far in the distance, a purple haze covering the slopes. Somewhere between here and there was Wallace, with all that money, plus what was probably a big bounty on his head. Limpy wondered how much. Too bad he couldn't extract that particular bit of information from the man back there in the distance. But it was too late now.

That stony-faced man—whoever he might be—was taking his chances, as they were taking theirs, and must suffer the consequences for his actions.

Up ahead the ground sloped sharply upward for more than one hundred yards to lip a ridge and then disappear beyond. Limpy could see the tracks of Wallace's two horses even at that distance, and when the party pulled up on top to blow their horses for a few moments the crippled man turned to Hornbuckle. Hornbuckle had the field glasses to his eyes again, as he had been doing at regular intervals since first discovering their pursuer.

"How far, Horn?" he asked.

"About three miles, I reckon. He don't seem to be in any particular hurry. Guess he must be pretty sure of himself."

Big Gert twisted her well built body in the saddle, straining her bosom against the man's shirt. Of them all she appeared to be the least fatigued.

"He's that kind," she said. "I've seen them before in the honky-tonks. I've a hunch he'll try to go around us tonight."

"He's not going anywhere past this ridge," Limpy grunted. "This is where he stops . . . for keeps. You all go on ahead just like natural. I'll wait here until he starts coming up and then slam him one good and center and bring in his horses. I'll pick up your trail and find where you're camped."

"Maybe I'd better stay with you," suggested One-Card. "Two's better than one."

Limpy almost sneered at him. "Since when did you ever learn to hit the side of a shed with a rifle? You'll get nervous fingers and throw one at him before he even gets in range. You trot along with the rest of them. I'll take care of him."

One-Card just as uglily sneered back: "And take whatever money he has, eh? Nice boy!"

"Cut it out, you men," ordered Hornbuckle, who had more or less assumed leadership aided by Big Gert. "Let's have no more of that."

Limpy rode over and extended a hand. "Better leave them glasses with me, Horn," he suggested.

He took them, raised them to his eyes, and adjusted them into focus. He studied the plain trail they were leaving, the surrounding terrain . . . and then slowly lowered them and looked at the others.

"That's funny," he said in a quiet voice, a queer note in it. "You seen anything besides that feller back there today, Horn? No? Well, I'da sworn I did just now. Seems like something moved over there about three quarters of a mile away, back of that ridge south and west of here."

Bart let go with one of his coarse bellows. "He's got buck fever, that's what. Plain buck fever. He gits ready to stop that tough hombre back there and then starts seein' things. Haw-haw-haw!"

"Have it your way," Limpy replied. He studied the terrain again, saw nothing this time, and lowered the glasses. "Better get going. I'll be along about sundown."

They left him there on the ridge and rode down the declivity on the other side. Limpy gigged his horse down about thirty yards and tied it securely to a greasewood bush. He took his rifle from the saddle boot and tucked a handful of cartridges into a pocket from his saddle bags. The climb back to the top sent fresh pain through his shortened, twisted leg, but to this he paid little heed now. He was going to kill a man. His third. The first in over twelve years.

There was another of the ubiquitous greasewoods growing right on the lip of the ridge, and behind this Limpy took cover, stretching himself out flat on his belly and piling up the extra cartridges within easy reach beside him. This was a mere precautionary move only, for the magazine of his repeater held four in the tube and one in the firing chamber, and the gun was fairly effective up to two hundred yards, its trajectory pretty flat to that distance. Limpy thought: I guess I oughta put his horse down first to make sure he don't get away. But if he barricades himself back of the carcass with that big .45-70 single shot Sharps I saw on his saddle, I'm liable to find myself in the position of the gent who caught the bear by the tail and couldn't let go. I couldn't get him but I couldn't run either. If I did I'd likely get one right through the back at a distance of four hundred yards.

He adjusted the field glasses again and watched the distant horizon, but Cogin had disappeared somewhere in the undulating swell of the desert. Limpy lay there and waited, using the glasses, that sense of uneasiness beginning to come over him again. He kept twisting around to watch the other ridges, some sixth sense telling him that there were others out there somewhere besides Cogin and himself.

Gosh, I'm getting jumpy, he thought. Guess it's only kind of natural after twelve years. I was younger then and hot-blooded. Didn't bother me a bit when I killed Della's stepfather and that tinhorn who rooked me at blackjack. And . . . shucks, this won't be any different. I got too much at stake to be worried. I wonder if she really *did* wait all these years. Well, I'll find out. . . .

He found the answer just forty-five minutes later, the answer that solved all his problems. He never knew just how they got so close upon him before he heard the first sound and turned his eyes from the fore. But what he saw chilled the blood in his veins and turned it to ice, and all the old terror of twelve years ago came back.

There were about twenty of them, the foremost not more than thirty feet away; lean, dark-skinned fellows in white muslin breech clouts and white deerskin leggings and moccasins. They were naked to the waist but with lateral streaks of white across their cheeks and noses just below the burning black eyes. Some wore bands of bright cloth around their heads. A few were armed with bows and arrows, the others guns; smooth bores and stolen .45-70 caliber Sharps Springfield rifles. Their leader was tall for an Apache, about twenty-eight, and instinct told Limpy who he was, why the patrol far to the north had not found him.

Nino. The Apache whose mother had been scalped by a white man.

Limpy stood there under their guns, the ice still in his veins, no doubt in his mind as to what would happen now. He knew. And he had no intention of letting them work on him.

With remarkable speed for a man of his type, he jerked his pistol free and shot himself through the side of the head.

Chapter 7

NINO LET out a grunt of contempt, and his moccasins and leggings made audible rustling sounds as he moved on up and stood looking down at the sprawled figure lying on its side. Nino rolled it over on its back and bent and picked up the rifle and pistol. The rest of the party had moved in close, one holding the reins of Limpy's horse.

"He would have died bad," the Apache said to the others, meaning that the White Eyes would have shrieked and yelled in pain instead of dying stoically like a strong man.

They went to work methodically, stripping the body of all clothing and valuables and then mutilating it with knives and lances. The saddle was taken from the dead man's horse and cut to pieces, all bits of metal such as cinch rings and buckles being saved, along with the bridle bit. Nino sat on the ridge with the glasses in his dark hands. They were the first pair he had ever seen, though he knew from past experience, plus what some of the scouts had told him, that the soldiers had some kind of magic eyes with which they could see as far or further than an Apache.

And now the glasses excited him. He squatted on his haunches, sweeping the hills and arroyos and ridges, small guttural sounds of wonder coming from him as far away objects came up close. He would look at a ridge, then jerk his eyes away and look again as it fell back into the distance, then bring it up close again and make more of those excited sounds.

The rest of his men had clustered around, some eager to look through the magic eyes but many clearly impatient to get after the others the party had spotted earlier that day. But Nino was in no hurry now. His last raid of a few days back, far to the north, had sent soldiers out from all forts as far north as Prescott, the regimental headquarters. The deserts and mountains were swarming with White Eyes, which was why he had streaked south and fled across the border into the land of the Me-hi-canos. He would give the White Eyes soldiers time to tire of the futile hunt and return to their forts to await another raid of Nino's choosing.

Down here he could rest and raid at leisure, for he held little fear of the Me-hi-cano soldiers. They fought only in the desert and would not venture into the mountains unless their numbers were as many as the blades of grass. Meanwhile Nino's new quarry of foolish White Eyes were heading in exactly the direction and directly toward the place he wished them to go. There was plenty of time.

They would kill the lone White Eyes who appeared to be trailing the others and let the others get into the mountains, where they could be taken alive. While the impatient younger warriors waited, Nino sat there on his haunches atop the ridge, the glasses glued to his dark eyes, and watched the back trail.

Sometime later he saw the man come into sight about a quarter of a mile distant. He was riding leisurely as though he had not a care in the world, like so many others of the stupid White Eyes. The rider came on closer, following the tracks of his quarry, and suddenly the expression on Nino's black face underwent a swift change He jerked the glasses down, raised them again, and that hissing intake of breath the Apaches uttered when excited now escaped him.

"Poco!" he exclaimed. "Poco!"

He turned his head and looked at an older warrior, the very brother of Tacana, the wrinkled scout Cogin had met that morning. The old man's black eyes were curious.

"It is Poco who comes," Nino said excitedly. "Poco the White Eyes who went back to his people twelve grasses ago when we raided the settlement among the cottonwood trees by the creek."

Poco. He had been dirty-faced and crying and shaking in terror when his new "father" brought him in from the raid on the Cogin ranch; and because he was so small they had named him Poco because the Apaches liked Spanish names. The sound was more musical on the Apache tongue, and it gave them a sense of superiority to take the names of their hated enemies.

I will show you how to play the Apache game of ball, White Eyes, and if you cry I shall beat you. You are an Apache now, and Apaches do not cry. . . .

He had shown the White Eyes and helped to teach him the Apache tongue. They had gone on summer hunting trips and run races and splashed in the cold streams and chased rabbits. They had become young novice warriors together until the time Nino saw Keneta go through the puberty rites and become a woman at fourteen grasses. The following summer, when she was fifteen grasses, Nino had led his three ponies over to the *jacal* of her parents one night and tied them there and crept away. All during the following day Keneta let them remain without watering them, as was customary.

But on the second day Nino had been in the brush at dawn, his eager eyes on the *jacal*. If she untied the horses and watered them there would soon be much dancing at a wedding feast. But if she refused . . .

He waited. The sun rose higher and still he waited. Perhaps she was sick, he told himself. Perhaps she had not seen the horses now tied there for more than thirty-six hours. His heart sank lower as the sun continued to climb, and at dusk, filled with shame and humiliation, he crept up and led the thirsty animals to water himself. His suit had been rejected.

Keneta preferred Poco. And Nino hated Poco for that.

"I'll beat her for that," Nino grunted to himself, the glasses now glued hard to his eyes while he studied Poco's features again. "I'll go back and tell her how I tortured Poco and then I'll beat her again."

He shifted on his haunches, his dark face expressionless, no sign of his thoughts visible. He thought: The White Eyes bullet did not cripple him. His arm swings good. If he had lifted the good arm that morning when we raided and he was shot, I could have dragged him up on my horse and he would still be an Apache. On the other hand, perhaps it was much better this way. Had Poco not been returned to his people Keneta now would be the mother of Poco's children instead of Nino's, as she now was.

It was better this way. He would capture Poco, torture him, and then go back and boast to Keneta while he beat her.

Nino put down the glasses. He picked up the repeating rifle that had belonged to Limpy, whose mulilated remains lay a short distance away, and examined it with satisfaction. He lined the sights on a distant rock, and they were straight and true to his eye. He turned to the others.

"When Poco comes near I'll shoot his horse dead and we'll take him alive," he said.

He lay down on his naked belly in the exact spot where Limpy had waited, and the warriors faded from the top of the ridge. Nothing showed up there as Cogin came on. He was wary from long experience but held little fear of trouble with the others up ahead. Like the Apaches, there was always plenty of time.

He dropped his horses down a bank to the sandy foot of the ridge and started up. One of the horses sneezed and blew dust from its nose. The pack pony walked along behind. It was late, and cooler now and quiet.

It was then that the shot came.

Cogin almost felt the bullet scream past his face as he heard the scream of the pack horse behind him. Nino, shooting down from above, and unused to the new rifle, had made the common mistake of so many who shoot down at a slant. He had fired high and killed the pack horse.

Cogin dropped the lead rope in a flash and wheeled, driving in the spurs hard. The bay leaped forward and began a rocketing run down the sandy floor of the arroyo while more shots came. Shrill yells came from above and in a matter of moments a group of about twenty or so Apaches spurred over the crest in a compact bunch. Cogin's left hand extracted a shell from his belt almost with the movement of his right as he jerked the huge single shot Sharps from its saddle boot. He wheeled in the saddle and drove a big slug of lead squarely into the group, killing a warrior.

He jerked the breech block open in a flash and inserted the second shell and slammed home another that killed a second warrior, went on through and wounded a third. That scattered them in all directions and made them poor targets now upon which to waste precious ammunition. Some wheeled and fled back over the ridge, others down toward where he had been fired upon. Nino and a few more spurred forward, firing wildly and trying to bring his horse down.

He had gained time in the initial dash as the band broke and scattered, and the light was still good yet for accurate shooting. Coolly he swung down and dropped to one knee. The big rifle went up and crashed back against his shoulder, and at a distance of almost three hundred yards he shot another one dead.

"Pull off, pull off!" screeched Nino, and followed it with a high-pitched yell that all understood. They fled like shadows and Cogin drove on, this time at an easy lope. An ordinary white man would have become panicked and run down an already tired horse. But Cogin was no ordinary man. He knew the Apaches.

They would try to get him in the darkness.

He trotted the horse, twisted in and out of gullies; playing for time that would bring on full darkness. When he had broken away he had wheeled to the left, heading in a northeast direction, making them believe he was running a circle to get around them. As a matter of fact, he did just the opposite.

He doubled back in the direction whence he had come and about nine that night returned to where the dead pack horse lay on its side. He didn't bother about removing the pack or salvaging anything from it. He could live on the land. The important thing was that he could hear their coyote signals far in the distance, and the way forward was now open. He led his horse up to the top of the ridge where the ambush had taken place, saw the mangled thing that lay there a vague lump in the darkness, and the long years he'd spent among those now out to capture him told a plain story.

"So they left Limpy behind to down me, and Nino caught Limpy instead," he said. "Afraid to share the 'reward' money for Wallace. And now I suppose I've got to save the damned fools' lives. Plus my own."

Chapter 8

COGIN SWUNG into leather again, left that mutilated thing on the ground to be finished off by the coyotes and buzzards, and rode slowly down the declivity. The calls were still coming from far away in the night, and those calls were asking if there was any trace of the White Eyes who had killed three of their number, wounded another, and escaped.

Cogin smiled to himself in the darkness. Some kind of a twisted fate that seemed to be enmeshing a lot of lives in a grim tangle of life and death had given him the knowledge and cunning to escape that first attack, to interpret their signals in the night, to know that if they tried to trail him in the darkness they would make slow progress.

He had no illusions as to what lay ahead, and you had to give Wallace credit for being either very frightened—which he most likely was not—or being a man of exceptional courage, which he was. He was heading straight for the Sierra Madre range, alone, into some of the wildest country on earth. A land of thousand-foot gorges and peaks, of puma and jaguar, of Mexican bandit robbers, of wild, fierce Indians, some of them other Apaches like those back there in the night.

Cogin thought: Wallace must not have known I was on his trail or he would have turned at bay.

He worked the horse on at a slow walk, partly so as to make less sound but mostly because it was cool and he wanted to conserve the animal's energy. The heat of traveling all day long across a burning desert takes much out of a horse, and nobody realized it more than

Cogin. Thus he let the animal take its own time while he sat with the big Sharps across his lap and watched the night and listened for sound. There was the usual call of the real coyotes, and now and then the spine-chilling roar of the big lobos that could hamstring a cow with one slash of their huge teeth and cut her throat with a second. An owl swooped by, sailing low above the greasewood, eyes on the ground for the long-tailed field mice that came out at night to feed.

Cogin covered a mile and then another, pulling up now and then to listen. Once his horse slobbered and he clamped a hand over its muzzle. He crossed an arroyo and climbed up a cut bank and began an ascent up a long, gentle slope. The ground would continue to rise from now on and would end, more than forty miles away, at the escarpment that was the foot of the great Sierra Madre range.

From somewhere up ahead, a mile further on, he caught a faint glow. He rode up onto a higher point, the instinct of the long years guiding him. He felt no need for caution until he saw the pin point of fire and knew he had found their camp.

He let the bay pick its way among the greasewood and cacti until at last he reached the small arroyo end one hundred yards above where the four of them were camped. The horse slid down the bank, and stones and dirt rattled. A voice in the distance called out, "That you, Limpy?"

He paid the call no heed but let the horse amble along the gravelly floor. He came into the light of the small fire and found four of them, three men and a woman, standing with ready rifles.

"Well, I'll be damned!" ejaculated Hornbuckle, lowering his gun. "The bounty hunter himself. I spotted you quite a way back. Had an idea you'd try to circle around us tonight and beat us to Wallace."

"Is that why you left Limpy behind?" Cogin asked sardonically as he swung down.

The woman Gert had not lowered her rifle at all. Even

in the dim light of the small fire Cogin could see her eyes back of the barrel's length; hard and determined but with just a touch of uneasiness in them.

"Drop that gun and then take off your belt, mister," she ordered. "So you got Limpy, eh? Drop that gun."

Cogin grunted and slid the Sharps back into its saddle boot. He ignored her and loosed the cinch on his saddle, shaking it to let air circulate between the blanket and the animal's sweaty back. He thought now that he should have taken time to cut open his pack from the dead carcass of the other mount and take out the grain sack. There was desert ahead for another day's ride, and there wouldn't be much forage nor the opportunity to let his tired mount hunt for it.

"Put down that gun and stop acting a fool," he ordered sharply.

He strode to the fire, aware of their hostility, their uncertainty. There were frying pans around where they had cooked flapjacks and bacon and made coffee from tins. He kicked the utensils aside and began using the side of his boot to scrape sand over the coals.

"Just a minute," broke in Bart belligerently. "What do you think *you're* doing? Where's Limpy?"

"He's dead," Cogin said, and went on covering the fire. The last of the coals disappeared and the camp was in darkness, in a desolate desert that sloped gradually upward toward the foot of the great Sierra Madres still so many miles away; four men and one woman who now must fight for survival.

Cogin sat down on a rock and reached for sack and papers, aware of the dim forms standing around him, the guns still lined toward where he sat.

"You'd better sit down and take it easy," he advised.

"We'll stand right here until we find out a few things, mister," the woman said. "And if you've got any idea that you get Limpy's share just because you killed him, you better think again."

"And you'd better forget Wallace for the moment,

lady," he answered quietly, spilling tobacco into the brown trough between his fingers.

Hornbuckle said just as quietly, "And you'd better do some explaining. I spotted you early today through my glasses, miles back. We didn't want you going around us tonight, so Limpy stayed behind to see you didn't. I don't know yet how you got by him. He was in perfect position for an ambush, and Limpy was a pretty good shot. You must have circled him and come in from behind."

"I didn't circle him. But some friends of mine did."

"Who?" demanded Bart, still belligerent.

Cogin said quietly, "Some Apaches led by an old friend of mine. Fellow named Nino."

"What!" cried out One-Card. "Apaches? Up here?"

"Down there," corrected Cogin quietly. "He wasn't a very pretty sight by the time they got through with him. Nino is good at that."

"So Limpy was right after all," Hornbuckle said thoughtfully. "He was nervous as a cat. Said he saw something, or thought he did. We figured it was buck fever at lining you up over a gun sight."

"They waited for me," Cogin went on in a matter-of-fact tone of voice. "About twenty of them. But the shot missed and killed my pack horse. We had quite a little fracas before I got away in the darkness and back-tracked to where they'd worked on him. As I said, Nino is good at that kind of thing."

"You think he's coming on after us?" asked the gambler, the fear in his voice expressing what lay in the hearts of all of them.

Cogin's grunt at such a simple question came through the darkness. He knew the workings of Nino's mind, his plans, just as clearly as though they had squatted down and talked as of old instead of slugging it out briefly in a running fight in which the raider had come off second best.

"He'll be after us," Cogin replied to the question, licking the cigarette paper. The match flared briefly, lit up his emotionless face for a brief moment over cupped hands, then died again as Cogin blew it out and let it drop between his booted feet. "The territory is hot for him now after the last series of raids. The country is covered by patrols of the kind you ran into. Hard-riding and willing but fighting them the West Point way, which is just what the Apaches want. Some of the scouts are doing their best, but others like the old fellow you saw with the patrol—his name is Tacana—are just drawing easy pay and not trying too hard. So Nino has come south into Mexico, where the Mexican troops are less persistent, to lie low for a while, raid down here, and hole up in the Sierra Madre. He's heading this way now to hole up. You fools are in front of him and can't turn back, and he's taking his time. He'll get you at his leisure . . . when he can take you alive."

His cigarette tip glowed brightly and then faded in the silence that followed. He heard the quick intake of breath of the fat man Bart and knew that sudden terror had struck home.

"You seem to know a lot about it," the woman finally said.

Cogin said, "I expect I do."

That was all that was said for a few moments. Cogin sat there and smoked the cigarette down to his fingers while he listened to them talk and discuss what to do next. Bart wanted to cut south again, try to circle around and find sanctuary in one of the villages or on a big hacienda in that green belt back there miles and miles away.

"They always have scouts out on each side, just out of gunshot range," Cogin informed him. "The moment you made a break for it, the main band behind would wheel over and come in for an attack."

"If there's not too many we could hole up and hold them off," suggested the gambler, the darkness covering the movement of that big lump in the front of his throat.

"And have them sit patiently day after day, emptying

bags of water in plain sight while your tongue swells with thirst. Dancing around and yelling. Using every form of torture they can think of. They'd love it. They don't like for a man to die quick and easy."

"So we're to be herded like sheep ahead of them into the mountains and slaughtered at their leisure?" demanded Hornbuckle.

"I reckon, mister," came Cogin's reply, "that that's about the size of it. I personally don't care what happens to any of you. Nobody asked you to come. You got yourself into this mess, and the only reason I'm staying with you for the moment is because in spite of my contempt and hatred for all of you, I'd like to see you have at least a part chance of getting away. I don't mind seeing all of you killed quick. None of you are fit to live. I just wouldn't want you to spend three days dying."

"Then what do you think we'd better do?" the woman asked, all antagonism gone from her now. In the brief time Cogin had known her, this was the first indication that beneath her exterior she was just a woman, after all; a very attractive woman, in fact.

"You'd better pack up and get out of here right away because they can trail by darkness. No trouble at all to follow the tracks of these horses in the sand. It'll take them three or four hours to find this camp but they'll find it, and some of those young bucks might be a little impatient to get to work. They might not wait."

He rose and dropped the butt of the cigarette and from force of habit ground it into the sand with his boot heel. "You better go pack up," Cogin told the silent group. "We've got a long ride ahead tonight and the horses are tired."

The horses were tired. You could feel it beneath you as they worked up out of the arroyo, hit the greasewood-studded wastes of the incline again, and went forward at a walk, carrying weight that was much heavier now than it had been when they were rested and early morning fresh.

Cogin led the way, the others following. Nobody spoke;

saddle leather creaked. The pack horses were being led by the man Bart. They traveled forward, climbing steadily, until the stars told Cogin that it was almost three o'clock in the morning.

He had always carried one water sack on his saddle, precaution against such events as had now come to pass. Now he unsaddled the tired animal, gave it most of the water from the sack, letting it drink out of his upturned hat, and took it to a place where bunch grass grew sparsely. The others watched and did the same. Then they slept the uneasy sleep of the tired, the hunted, the cornered.

At sundown the following day they came to a halt, after a long final climb, where a spring gurgled down through some rocks; where the grass was green and, above them, were steep timbered slopes.

On the far reaches of the plain below nothing moved in the desert. Nothing.

Nothing that was visible to the human eye.

They're waiting, Cogin thought. They are in no hurry.

Chapter 9

ONE OF the many phenomena of the desert is the remarkable suddenness with which a rainstorm can come up. The sky is listless, flat-looking, and glaringly bright in the dry heat. Half an hour later a change is felt in the air, and then the first clouds begin to form. Cogin saw them as the party made camp.

He was unsaddling his horse near where Hornbuckle was doing the same. He said, "You'd better have your people make camp over there in the clearing away from the trees."

Hornbuckle paused, and the instinct of fear caused him subconsciously to throw his gaze back down the long slope to where there still was no moving object in sight.

"You think they'll try it tonight, eh?"

Cogin shrugged. "I was thinking of lightning near these trees. It's dangerous. But the rain will blot out tracks, and that might give us some temporary help."

"Rain?"

"In about two hours . . . and lots of it. Better make your camp accordingly."

He hoped they all had sense enough to construct some small brush *jacals* and then cover them with their waterproof bedroll tarps. As for himself, this thing of spending a night in a storm without shelter was nothing new. The Apaches never bothered with such cumbersome things as big bedrolls, and for that reason he did not feel too keenly the loss of his own pack. He was pretty certain that Wallace was not too far ahead, and he wanted to go after him before the rain started, trailing him as far as possible before the man's trail was blotted out.

Cogin picketed his horse at the end of the lariat and carried his saddle with its empty water sack and saddle bags toward the lee side of a big rock. The others were busy doing the same. The woman Gert came over and flung down her bedroll and sat down on it with a bit of a tired sigh. She removed first her hat and gloves and then the weighty cartridge belt.

"Got a match on you?" she asked, reaching for tobacco sack and papers. "I'm so tired I could drop, and a cigarette will taste good. I could even go a small drink right now if there was one handy."

"There is," Hornbuckle replied. "I slipped in an extra pint for just such an occasion. Might be the last time we'll ever have a chance to take one, too, come to think of it," he added with wry attempt at humor that fell completely flat.

The gambler One-Card was already picking up a good-sized rock and placing it next to another preparatory to starting the evening cook fire. Cogin handed the woman the match and told them all to get their cooking done before dark, use a small fire that made little or no smoke, and then to take turns at night guard with the horses bunched up close.

He had already sat down and was removing his boots. Gert watched him over the smoke of her brown paper cigarette, watched the play on his lean face as he tugged off first one and then the other.

"You know, Charley, you could be almost human if you wanted to," she remarked with an attempt at real friendliness. He had told them only that his name was Charley and let it go at that. Nor did Hornbuckle as yet even dimly ever suspect that this man they all hated, yet now looked forward to for leadership, was the same "Apache" Hornbuckle had stood over that morning of the raid on the settlement.

Cogin didn't answer the woman. He had opened up his saddle bags and removed a pair of moccasins. These he slipped on his feet and laced the strings around his ankles. Bart came over, puffing a little, some dry brush in his arms. He tossed it down beside the two rocks, straightened, and wiped the sweat from his face.

"Dog-gone but it's hot," he grunted. "This mountain country is a lot different from down there in the desert. I was allus told that the mountains are cool, but up here I can hardly draw muh breath."

"You'll be cool enough in a very short time," Cogin said. "And soaking wet."

The others had begun eyeing him coolly and suspiciously now as he took some jerky from a saddle bag and stuffed it into his pockets. The woman Gert rose to her feet as he removed the huge Sharps rifle from the saddle boot.

"Where do you think you're going?" she demanded roughly.

"After Wallace. His tracks show that he can't be too far

ahead. I want to get on them before the rain washes them out."

"So . . ." The woman again, her lips thin and cold where but moments before they had been smiling as she watched him. "Still want all of that money for yourself, plus all the bounty, too, eh?" she jeered. "Just going on up alone to knock him off and take everything. Then you'll lay out there hidden in the brush and wait for the Apaches to finish us off. Or were you going to take Wallace's horses and beat it on alone?"

He looked at every one of them, the tense positions of their bodies, the greed and suspicion and fear. The contempt for them lay plain in his eyes.

"There's no reward money on Wallace's head," he informed them quietly. "And the other money will be returned to the banks, the rightful owners. You invited yourselves on this little party and now there'll be no money of any kind for any of you. The one thing you'd better concentrate on now is just getting back alive. I know Nino and how his mind works. If his impatient young bucks don't talk him into letting them work on you tonight, they'll probably wait until we get still higher into the wild country. I told you he has plenty of time. He'll pick the strongest one of you—probably you, Hornbuckle—and work on you for about two to three days until you finally go under. You two men will follow second and third. They'll save the woman for the last, and probably swing her head down by her heels over a slow fire."

"My God!" whispered Bart, his flabby, sweating face the color of cold ashes. "Them devils can't do that to us. We got to git outa here. We got to!" His voice rose to a higher pitch and ended almost in a wild cry.

"That's why I'm going after Wallace," Cogin said curtly. "To bring him back here, not to kill him. We'll need every extra gun we can get to pull out of this mess."

He shifted the rifle, automatically making sure of the ugly snouted length of brass in the firing chamber, and Hornbuckle, the calmest of the four, spoke again. He was eyeing Cogin quietly, speaking quietly.

"Then just why *are* you trailing him?"

Cogin gave him back a level-eyed look. "He stopped over at our ranch in Kansas for two or three days and went head over heels for a sister of mine twice as young as he is. When she wouldn't run off with him he lost his head and got rough. She's dead now, and Wallace will probably pay for it staked out on the ground or tied to a post. I have no intention of letting him ride on while we protect him from the rear. You keep a double guard of two all night, lying flat on the ground, feet to feet. Keep the horses bunched up close and watch them; listen for nervous slobbers. They can smell an Apache, and they don't like it any more than an Indian pony likes a white at first. I'll get back with Wallace in tow as soon as possible. If I don't make it in time I'll bury what's left of you."

"You got us into this, damn you!" the woman accused him. "It was all your fault. You come in there trailing Wallace and not telling anybody anything. And because of you we're hemmed in by a bunch of bloodthirsty Apaches that you seem to know one whale of a lot about."

"I do," he replied calmly. "I was raised with Nino for eleven years. We're enemies, and my presence here will please him very much. That's why I know what we're up against."

"Wait a minute!" cried out Hornbuckle. "That raid on the settlement years ago! That Cogin kid—he—you—no, it can't be! *It just can't be!*"

"It's true, I reckon," was the reply. "I'm Cogin. I'm the man who shot Limpy's leg from under him that morning twelve years ago. I'm kind of glad he got his before he had a chance to find out who I am . . . or was. Well, now you know. I'll do whatever I can and use whatever knowledge I haven't forgotten to get you out of this mess. But don't depend upon it. There's about sixteen of them in the band, but they can get more with smoke signals if they get us cornered and need help."

He shifted the heavy rifle to his other arm, knowing that he might be seeing them alive for the last time. The thought gave him neither satisfaction nor sorrow, merely a feeling of contempt for the greed they had shown for an opportunity to collect blood money, where there had been no bounty money at all. He didn't hate them any more than he hated Wallace. He neither loved nor hated any person alive. And that included Nino. They were merely enemies of long standing.

A slight breeze swept through the surrounding trees as though some invisible giant were fanning the green foliage with his hand. It waved gently back and forth, back and forth. Down on the desert more than twenty dust devils, or small whirlwinds, were funneling their way across the wastes. The air seemed to grow more humid. Hornbuckle cleared his throat and spoke.

"Just in case you don't get back tonight, what do we do?"

"Keep climbing as near due east as possible and cover as much ground as you can. If you go far enough you'll find thousand-foot gorges; it will take you three days just to find a way to the bottom. You'll come up against mountains you can't climb even on foot. Do the best you can, keep a sharp lookout all the time, and double guards at night. Don't kill any game with a gun, because there's more up here than Apaches and just as bad. Mexican bandit gangs; renegade American outlaws who raid mines and mule trains; bands of Mexican army deserters . . . plus a few things like grizzlies, jaguars, rattlesnakes and scorpions. If the rain blots out your tracks I'll cut them again, never fear about that."

He said it in a matter-of-fact way as though they had been discussing the price of sheep or cattle. Then he turned and was moving away, a solitary figure in moccasins; alone, indifferent, still aloof.

He disappeared up the slope just as the spine-chilling roar of a lobo wolf came floating down on the breeze.

Chapter 10

THE WIND began to increase in velocity, whipping at the brush and berry patches and the green branches of the trees; coming down from above as though to meet and join with the storm forming on the wastes of the desert miles below. Cogin saw antelope bounding away, and deer by the dozens. A few broke and ran, followed by long-legged fawns; others stood and watched him curiously. An eight-point buck moved forward belligerently, followed him a few yards, and then turned back.

For that Cogin was grateful to the buck. He wanted no shot to warn Wallace of his presence or others who might be lurking within sound of a gun. But he could tell from the animals' actions that there was a heavy storm in the offing, and he moved on as fast as he could climb steadily. He saw far among the distant mountain ranges a small black cloud that was pouring a dark mass of rain on some isolated spot, and he knew that down among the canyons and gorges the wind was howling. The *zopilotes*—the great black-necked Mexican buzzards—so plentiful an hour ago, had now disappeared completely; gone back to their caves and their young to sit out the storm in darkness, croaking and groaning like tortured souls of the dead.

Cogin covered the first three miles before the rain drops began to fall, slanting down from above. He cursed inwardly because the tracks of Wallace's two horses were still plain and easy to follow; they were fresh enough to indicate that the man couldn't be much further ahead. Probably holed up in shelter to ride out the storm.

A rustle in a nearby berry patch caught his eyes and ears at the same time, and a big she-bear raised up on her hind legs to peer at him. Then the thing he most feared happened: with a rumbling growl she crashed through and lunged straight at him. He thought: Blast the luck! I was afraid of something like this.

He let her get within twenty feet of him, coming at full charge with the red mouth and flaming eyes wide open. The .45-70 caliber bullet caught her squarely in the mouth, and he leaped aside as she rolled past him and two big cubs let out bleating cries and fled away together.

The heavy roar of the big single shot went rolling away into the distance. It rolled far away down the slopes whence he had come and struck faintly but unmistakably the ears of three men and a woman who jumped to their feet and looked at each other with a mute question in their eyes.

It brought Wallace out of his tarp shelter, where he had holed up comfortably, to stare with that same question in his eyes.

It struck faintly at the ears of the bandit Victorio Lopez and eight of his tough followers camped two miles away.

Cogin stood there levering out the smoking shell and shoving in another, his lips tight and grim. He knew the four back in camp must have heard the shot and might become panicky. He wondered if Nino was far back in the desert or if, watching the camp of the four, the Apaches had heard it too.

But there was nothing to do but go on now. If he went back to the camp Wallace might become frightened and escape. If he went on . . . Cogin went on. The rain was wetting his shirt and shoulders, but he paid it no heed, just as Nino and his warriors, without shelter, would pay it no heed.

The ground was becoming a bit slippery in the bare spots now, and a few tiny rivulets began to run. He doubted if this particular downpour would last too long. It was another of those so typical of the country.

He lost the tracks just as darkness began to crowd down onto dusk, and there was nothing to do but find shelter and sit out the night. If the rain ceased by morning Wallace would move on and Cogin could cut a two or three mile circle and pick up the tracks of the two horses again.

But by then it would probably be too late to get back to aid the others. Nino, if Cogin gauged him right, would strike about tomorrow night, and it would be doubtful if there would be that much time.

Cogin covered another mile in the rain, which was now beginnng to lessen. It was still light enough to see some distance, for in summer the sun does not set up there until about eight o'clock. There was a cluster of rocks ahead; big white fellows standing up eight feet high. Cogin made for them, to get on the lee side and hunker down and eat jerky. He half slipped and slid in the mud down a three-foot bank and almost lost his balance.

He saw the brush shelter, the tarp over it, the two picketed horses. He heard Wallace's voice from behind:

"Drop the gun, Charley, and then unbuckle your belt with your left hand."

Cogin lifted his blank eyes and saw Wallace. The fugitive he had trailed more than fifteen hundred miles sat on his haunches on a rock some four feet above, elbows resting on his knees, a big pistol in each hand. From a corner of his mustache a cigarette trailed smoke up past one eye.

There was nothing for Cogin to do but obey the command. He knew this man too well, his past record of coming off victor in gun duels that had taken the lives of nineteen men both good and bad, the man's cold courage. He placed the rifle against a rock, leaning it barrel up, and unbuckled his belt and let the heavy object drop to the ground. Wallace slid down the rock as Cogin stepped away from reach of his weapons.

"Well, I'm glad it's over, Charley," Bas Wallace said

quietly. "You'll never know the torture I've suffered all these weeks, the nights when every sound of a wood rat was your boots in the darkness . . . you with a gun in your hand like I've got one now."

"Why didn't you turn on me?" Cogin asked carelessly. "I'm no gun fighter and you are."

Wallace was backing a few feet away, one gun still covering Cogin, his eyes never leaving Cogin's face. He knelt beside his shelter, reaching back of him to fumble at his pack. "If I'd thought it was just that, Charley, I wouldn't have hesitated. I'd have stopped off in some town and got you . . . even if I'd had to do it in the back."

"Then why didn't you?" was the harsh question.

"Because," Wallace said quite frankly and honestly, his eyes glinting, "I was afraid of you. I still am. You wasn't the kind to ride into a town in the open when you figgered I was there. Not a man who was raised among the 'Paches. *That's* what I was afraid of, Charley. The 'Pache in you."

Cogin thought bitterly, Yes, I know. I know all about it. The thought suddenly filled him with smoldering anger at his father.

Howdy, stranger. Light and rest a spell. I'm Lee Cogin. Wallace? Never heard of you but glad to meet you. This is my son Charley, foreman of my outfit. Mebbe you heard of him, eh? Used to live with the Apaches. Yessir, they got him when he was five an' kept him 'leven years. Couldn't speak a word of English when we got him back, but he can shore trail a centipede across lava rock.

Damned old fool, why don't he shut up? Why does he always have to keep boasting and blowing about something a man wants to forget?

Pap, for Pete's sake, why do you have to keep bringing it up every time a stranger comes to this ranch? I know I'm a freak among these plains people up here, but why do you have to keep making it worse? I never saw this

Wallace visitor before and I don't expect he gives a damn where I was raised, since he don't expect ever to see me again. So, for Pete's sake, lay off, will you?

Why, shucks, son, it ain't nothin' to be ashamed of, even if you are different from the rest of us. I just thought it might sorta explain that funny accent you talk with an' keep 'em from starin' at you. . . .

"Ah, here they are," Wallace said in satisfaction, and brought out two objects. A pair of handcuffs and a badge now partly rusted. Wallace looked at them and laughed. "Do you know what, Charley? I've carried these for so many years I've forgotten; outa habit, I suppose. Just never got around to throwing them away after I gave up being a peace officer. And now they come in handy against the one man in this world that I've been afraid of."

He opened the cuffs and tossed them to Cogin. "Fasten them to your wrists in front, Charley. That way you can roll smokes and eat. There's no hurry about the job we both know I've got to do. And for some strange reason I'd kinda like to explain to you what actually happened up there at the ranch. Maybe I ain't as bad a man as some people think. By the way, what would you have done if you'd caught me flat-footed here in camp."

Cogin was busy putting the rusty cuffs on his own wrists. He nodded down the slope to where, about forty feet away, a large mound rose up out of the ground near the rotted trunk of a big tree probably felled by lightning many years before.

He said, "I'd have buried you up to your neck in one of those and waited for the sun to come out in the morning."

Wallace stared at him, and when he spoke his voice almost a whisper. "You would do *that?* To a white man? Even *you?*"

"An Apache like me wouldn't have done what you did in Kansas," Cogin said without emotion. "It was against tribal laws and religion to molest an unmarried girl against her will."

But he knew that what he had said was untrue. That

might have happened had it not been for the chain of circumstances that had brought the lives of others into his own plans, enmeshed them, and twisted them into a pattern that would probably explode into deadly violence. And Wallace's guns would have come in handy.

Wallace still had him covered, and now he removed Cogin's weapons to the opposite side of the camp, secured a lariat and piggin string, and came back. He tied one end around Cogin's chest just below the armpits, knotting the rope from behind, and then fabricated with the piggin string a makeshift harness that held the prisoner's arms below his shoulders. A stunted tree grew between two of the rocks above, and to its lone limb the fugitive fastened the other end of the picket rope.

When he was finished he stepped back and eyed his work with satisfaction. Cogin could move his cuffed hands up and down to a limited extent, could reach the fire but no further. Only then did Wallace sheath his gun and step back.

"All right, Charley," he said in satisfaction. "That'll take care of you while I cook us some swell supper. Fresh venison steaks."

Cogin had backed up against the perpendicular face of one of the rocks, sheltering himself from the rain now pelting them less harshly. "You must have been pretty confident . . . using a gun that I might have heard," he pointed out.

Wallace laughed. "Give me credit for having some sense, Charley. It was a young deer that a big catamount had just filled up on. I chased him away and cut off a few choice chunks. And speaking of shots, was that yourn I heard?"

Cogin nodded and told him about the she-bear, and all the terrible tenseness that had been bottled up inside Wallace during the past weeks now flooded out in his laugh of sheer relief.

"That was really a break for me. I've been ducking and dodging for so long the shot came as a relief, though it meant bad news: either you, one of the bandit gangs I spotted yesterday, or Apaches. There's plenty of all of them, but I had to take a chance alone through here, hoping that some of them would stumble onto you and take you off my hands."

"They're still going to," Cogin said. "Nino and some of his best warriors are down below looking after some friends of mine—" sardonically—"and one of yours. The woman called Big Gert."

Chapter 11

THE RAIN was still pelting down, the wind whipping through the trees on the ridge above. Dark clouds scuttled and roiled as though romping in the back yard of the sky, gleefully; playing tag above. The two horses on picket ropes stood with hips acock, the traditional posture of horses at rest; bearing the wetness in patience. Cogin braced himself against the rock. Wallace was crawling beneath his tarp shelter to get at a dry shirt.

"Night owls and bald eagles!" he grinned, turning and sitting down on dry earth, stretching his legs out before him. "You don't say? And just why should that bunch of unholy characters be down here?"

Again Cogin went into detail. Something about it seemed to arouse amusement in the man. He went off into laughter, the mustache that drooped completely over his mouth and covering it from sight waving like wheat stalks before a wind.

"You don't say? Big Gert herself, eh? She didn't fool me in the least, playing up to me like she did. That gal is the practical type. But she wouldn't play ball in my league even after I baited her with promises to come back some day and set her up in a gambling hall."

"Didn't you intend to?" asked Cogin carelessly; anything to make idle conversation. He was completely disinterested.

Wallace laughed again, fumbling for the clean, dry shirt. "I never intended coming back, Charley. Back in the states and territories I'm supposed to be just another badman. But I've known for quite some time that my string was just about played out up there. It started in Texas, right after the Civil War, when I was an officer with two Negro deputies. I needed a stake to set up in Mexico and I got one. No, Charley, I didn't intend to go back to Big Gert. It's Mexico for me."

"I guess she must have figgered that one out when she came after you," Cogin said wryly. "A woman like her might, after working in dance halls and gambling joints and under suspicion as to how her husband died."

"I guess so. She didn't fool me. Anyhow . . . so they got the jump on you and came after me for money. And then you got the jump on *them* and came after me to put me in an ant hill."

"That was to come later, if Nino didn't get the upper hand. I had no intention of killing you now. I came after you because I needed your guns. I still do . . . if you've got sense enough to know what's best for you."

Wallace paused, in the act of stripping off his wet shirt. "Come again?"

"Nino knows we're following another man because he can read tracks like you can read a letter or newspaper. He knows you're not far ahead. The six of us together might have a chance. If those four dumb sheep down there face it alone, after you kill me, Nino will get them and he'll get you too. You better turn me loose, Wallace. You need me as much as I need your guns. If you kill me you'll have around sixteen tough Apaches on your trail who know this country better than any white man. They'll get you and you won't die easy. I've seen Nino work before."

Wallace had the wet shirt off by now and the dry one in his hands. The rain was still pelting off Cogin's shoulders even in the lee of the rocks. It kept whipping around in gusts and changing direction.

Wallace appeared to ponder a moment, then slowly shook his head. He grinned a bit. "No go, Charley. This rain will blot out tracks and give me plenty of start while this Nino occupies his time with them four money hunters. I'll have plenty of time. Would you like to see that money? Here it is."

He lifted two canvas sacks from the bag. The sacks were rounded out but soft-looking . . . as though wadded with paper.

The rain ceased as suddenly as it had come. The clouds roiled on and the wind began to die down. Wallace proved his knowledge of woodcraft by bringing from beneath the tarp shelter a pile of dry brush he had provided and began to build a fire. He had some beans and boiled potatoes in onionskin sacks, and these he heated while the deer steaks broiled over the coals. They ate mostly in silence, finished the meal, and Wallace cleaned the utensils. It was about ten-thirty by now. The sky was clear.

"I'm going to turn in and get a fresh start in the morning, Charley," the fugitive told Cogin. "Sometime before daylight. You'll have to make out the best you can, which shouldn't be hard for a man who's lived among the Apaches. When I get ready to go I'll make it as easy as possible for you. After all," pointing down to the ant hill, "I'm a *white man*."

He put both his and Cogin's weapons beside his blankets and lay down, but did not remove his boots. He stretched out on his back, hands back of his head, and watched the handcuffed man by the big rock. Cogin had squatted down on his haunches. He sat there; silent, without emotion, somber eyes gazing into the now dying fire; sat there like an Apache.

Wallace thought: We're two of a kind, him and me. We don't hate each other or anybody else. Just two of a kind. The small things like love and a family and kids and respect of the ignorant in some two-bit community are beneath us. Just two of a kind. . . .

He pulled up in front of the small, drab building where the horses of the four men stood racked, swung down and looked up at the two Negro deputies. They were big fellows, they were newly freed, they carried the law on their shirt fronts, and they were led by a man who had a reputation for fearlessness. All three carried big brass-bound Dragoon revolvers.

"Eb, you and Tom follow me to the door but don't come in," Wallace said. "I'll try to take them without trouble if possible."

The two deputies got down and obeyed. Wallace stepped to the porchless building, warped and cracked after four years of abandonment during the war. He moved into the drab interior, decorated only by a crude bar and some equally crude chairs and table. There were six men inside. Four of them had been trailed here. The shadows of the two Negro deputies darkened the door behind his broad young back.

The owner back of the bar moved ominously forward; a Texas soldier of the Confederacy who had just lost a fight and was still filled with hatred and plain, sullen bitterness.

"You git them dam' badge-packin' niggers outa here, mister," he snapped.

"They'll stay in," Wallace said tonelessly; and to the four men, calling them off by name: "I have warrants for your arrest for horse stealing. Get up and come quietly and there will be no trouble."

None of them spoke. They sat there, tough men of the Texas brush country. They too had helped to free the two Negro deputies who now had come after them. They warily eyed Wallace and the two, and waited.

The owner said savagely, "I don't give a dam' whether you want 'em for hoss thievery, baby stealin' or wife beatin'. But there ain't no dam' carpet-bagger Nawther an' two black men takin' anybody outa this place, so git! Git!"

"They stole the horses from poor people," Wallace explained patiently; "people like yourself who are trying to get a fresh start after the war. And now they can walk out on their feet or get packed out feet first."

Three of them had been packed out feet first after the roar of the old brass-bound pistols had subsided and the gunsmoke of old-fashioned powder cleared away. The two Negro deputies hadn't needed to be packed out; they lay sprawled in the dirt, stone dead—shot out of the open doorway. And that alone was all that enabled Wallace to escape. He managed to get on his horse, his own gun gone, because the slug from a cap-and-ball was buried deep in his right shoulder and the hole it made was bleeding profusely. He went down the street at a run, humped low over his horse, bullets from the Henry rifle of the cursing, frantically shooting saloon owner whizzing all around him. All thirteen of them.

And Wallace, young as he was, was too prudent and intelligent to go back, even to remain in that part of the turbulent state that was still shaking itself savagely to clear up the wounds of the war they had helped to loose. He had been twenty-three then, fourteen years ago, in 1866, and he had shot the three of them without warning before the other three and the owner got into action; partly because he was an officer determined to take them and mostly because of the same ungovernable temper that had harried him down through the years.

The saloon with its three dead white man inside and two dead black men outside faded, and he saw faces come out of the past and pass in review: the woman he had married and then left with child, dance hall girls; the faces of men crumpled before him, lax in death. He saw the piquant face of bold-eyed, flirtatious Jenny Cogin, who had led him on, teasing him by letting him smile and make eyes at her; she who had paid with her life by inflaming an ungovernable temper, the only emotion in Wallace's black soul.

He thought: Why should a man's soul be white anyhow? I like it better this way. Big Gert. I think I missed out on a good bet there, because she's the kind of woman for men like Charley sitting over there and me. So maybe I'll change my mind. Maybe I won't go to Chihuahua City. Maybe if she gets out of this I'll go back to the settlement and get her. . . .

A yawn broke off his thoughts and he stirred beneath the shelter. "See you in a few hours, Charley," he called, and closed his eyes.

Chapter 12

COGIN MADE no reply, squatting there on his haunches as immobile as the rocks themselves. He couldn't climb the rope because it was impossible to get his hands above his head. So he sat there as the last of the coals became ashes and the wild animal sounds came floating through the wild, rugged country and Wallace's gentle, regular breathing came to his ears.

Then he began to chew on the rope.

It was, luckily, not of iron hard rawhide but a manila type made in Mexico from the fibers of the maguay plant. They cut into his mouth and caused the blood to begin flowing, but to this Cogin paid no heed. He held it between his manacled hands, head bent low, gnawing at it like some wild animal. The fibers finally began to give way under his teeth and saliva that made them soft, and he began to tear at it almost savagely.

One of the dozing horses suddenly raised its head and gave off a soft, uneasy slobbering noise. Cogin raised up, his body tense, a cold chill that was not from his wet clothing going through him. The slobber came again and he strained frantically at the few remaining strands as he saw the movement out there. He thought: I've got to get free. I can't let Nino stake me out after what happened years ago.

"Wallace!" he whispered sibilantly. "Wallace! Wake up! They're here!"

He didn't know whether that thing out there, crawling forward like a thick-bodied timber rattlesnake, had seen him or heard him. He knew only that it was there, coming in on the camp, that he was tied and helpless to get at a gun.

"Wallace!" he roared in a ringing cry, a cry that rent the black night and went slashing down below to come back with an echo. "Wallace! Get out of there quick!"

It was then that the dark object beyond the horses sprang erect and dived at the two mounts, and even in the night Cogin saw the knife in its hand. The horses reared in fright as the two ropes were cut and then went plunging and snorting down below with rocks clattering beneath their hoofs. A mocking laugh came floating back as Wallace leaped out, pistol in hand.

"What is it?" he demanded.

His answer came in that mocking laugh again, followed by bold words in Spanish. "The name is *El Señor* Victorio Lopez, the bandit, *señores*. I will talk with you tomorrow."

Wallace stood there for a moment as though in indecision, and then stumbled over to where Cogin stood. "That sounded like Spanish," he said. "I can only speak a half-dozen words."

'I'm darned glad it wasn't Apache," grunted Cogin. "That's what I thought when I first saw him crawling up. I tried to call you but you were dead to the world. I had to yell."

The sounds of the horses were still coming from below, and Wallace, the temper that had caused him so much misfortune during his earlier years set afire, lifted his pistol and drove three shots down the slope, the foot-long orange flames lighting up briefly the night around them.

"That's fine," Cogin said bitterly, bitingly, as the mocking laughter rose in chorus all around them. "Go right ahead. Tell Nino and his men exactly where we are."

Wallace grunted a sour curse at the rebuke, turning, the gun dangling at his leg. He said in the darkness, "Well, it looks like we're afoot and surrounded by some two-bit Sierra Mexican outlaw and his men. That much I could understand. Now what do we do?"

"You can cut me loose and give me my guns," Cogin said harshly. "He said he'd talk with us in the morning. But if he had been ten minutes later I'd have been free and we'd be on our way back down to where those four scared sheep are waiting for mine and your guns. You better cut me loose. We're both in the same boat now, and after that shooting—with no horses—things are going to get worse. That bandit will probably hold us here just long enough for Nino and his men to finish off the woman and her three companions, and then come on and wind up the rest of it. I know Nino. I was raised with him. If he hits their camp tonight and finds me gone after you, he'll take as many prisoners as possible and be hot on our trail. And the great Mexican bandit, *el Señor* Victorio Lopez—" bitterly—"will accommodatingly hold us here for a final grand Apache party. Cut me loose, you damned fool!"

Wallace did not hesitate. He took his sheath knife and cut the rope at the chewed spot, a slight grunt of surprise coming from him. He used a key to unlock the rusty handcuffs and Cogin went to the shelter. He slung his waist cartridge belt around him and then put on the other that Wallace had previously removed while tying him up. Stoically he took his big rifle and went back to the place where he had been squatting.

"You seem to be pretty good at climbing rocks," he pointed out to the man who was no longer his captor but a companion. "I'll watch the east side, down the slope. You take the west."

They took up their respective positions, Cogin with his back to the perpendicular side of the rock, looking in one direction, to the east; Wallace four feet above, watching the darkness to the west. The coyotes howled and the lobos gave off their harsh roars, and accompanying the sounds came the sounds of much gleeful laughter somewhere out there in the now chilly night. Neither of the two men spoke or smoked during the vigil. It grew bitingly cold in the early morning hours, and Cogin's wet clothes, like ice now, sent shivers through his body.

He saw the first signs of daybreak, a light curtain pulled across the distant mountain tops toward which he sat facing, and then he saw smoke far down below. *Señor* Lopez, it appeared, was up and around for an early breakfast.

"We might as well eat," Cogin said to Wallace, and rose to stretch the kinks from his knee joints and shake some of the cold out of his frame. "Smoke from the fire will give them the idea we're not too worried. Once I convince that two-bit bandit that Nino and his warriors are due any time now today, it'll be the great *Señor* Lopez's turn to start worrying. You keep watch. I'll build the fire."

He built it between two rocks, and because the wood was wet it threw up a long, thin plume of grey smoke tinged with yellow. A voice from far down below, carrying easily through the distance separating the two smoke plumes, floated up to them—mocking, derisive.

"Hey, *señores,* maybe you slept pretty good last night, eh?" It was followed by a small chorus of coarse guffaws.

Wallace, atop the tallest of the rocks in the cluster, cursed.

"Let him laugh," Cogin said. "Nino will get the last one . . . on all of us."

"Don't say a thing like that," snapped Wallace. His face was unshaven, tired, drawn, the strain of the night's vigil showing. "I don't mind getting killed off if I got to go sudden like. I've expected something like it for years. Every time I moved in on a man for a final showdown that meant one of us was going to die, I was all tight and maybe scared inside, but I wasn't afraid because I knew if I got it it would come plenty sudden. But this kind of thing . . . trapped this way. Bottled up and waiting for a bunch of Apaches. . . ."

He cleared his throat, coughed, spat savagely against the side of a rock.

They ate big chunks of the half raw deer meat, broiled over the fire's live coals, smoked cigarettes. Half an hour later the distant voice, closer now, hailed them again. It came from behind a rock some two hundred yards away.

"Hey, *señores,* do you speak Spanish?"

"What do you want?" Cogin called back in the same language.

"I want to talk with you. Maybe you come down and talk with me, eh? Victorio Lopez is an honorable man. I will not try to trick you."

"I'll meet you halfway," Cogin answered. "In the open."

"Very well. But no tricks. I have many men with me."

Cogin turned to Wallace. "What kind of a rifle have you got?"

"A fifty-six caliber Spencer. Seven shots from the tube magazine in the stock, and I've got two spare tubes. I can throw out twenty-one shots pretty fast."

"It's not worth a dam' for range, but you shouldn't miss at a hundred yards. Cover me while I go down. He wants to *habla*. If they try anything, get this Lopez first and then use my forty-five seventy to make it hot for the others at long range. Army sharpshooters have hit a man at a thousand yards with one of these guns, using that new-fangled telescope sight."

He left his belt and rifle with Wallace and came out into the open, moving down across ground that sloped gently, the rawhide soles of his moccasins making no sound in the grass. He had to leap a three-foot wide chasm thirty feet deep in the earth, and he wondered idly if it had been caused by a cave-in of one of the old lost Spanish *Conquistadore* mines worked by Indian slaves or if there was an earthquake fault running through here.

The thought left his mind as a man in white cotton

shirt and pants, boots and big straw sombrero, rose into sight and came to meet him.

"Ah, greetings, *señor*. It pleases me much to see you this fine morning after the rain. And now we talk, eh? I am the great bandit, *Señor* Victorio Lopez."

Chapter 13

HE STOOD there with his legs braced apart, in all his self-importance and self-glory, a really great, veteran bandit . . . all of twenty-five years of age. Certainly no more than twenty-six; illiterate, boastful, confident. Crisscrossed over his shoulders were two bandoliers carrying a type of odd-looking cartridge, probably for a rifle of German or Austro-Hungarian make that had found its way across the broad Atlantic and, by devious methods, ended up in the fastness of the wild Sierra Madre—the Mother Mountain. In the hands of a man who believed himself to be really great. His inch-long black whiskers grew in sparse patches along his cheeks, at the upper corners of his mouth, at the point of his chin. Under other circumstances he would have appeared ludicrous.

"What do you want?" Cogin asked curtly. "Talk fast and get it over with. You're covered with a rifle from up above. If you try any tricks my friend will shoot you down like a dog."

"And you, too, my friend," laughed the other.

He stood there looking at Cogin, weighing shrewdly what lay back of the blank face of this tall *norteamericano*. A tough one, this one. And not afraid either. Not like the simple villagers he and his men terrorized to get food and horses.

"What do you want?" Cogin repeated harshly.

Lopez spread his hands expansively and shrugged. "We are but poor peons, *señor,* who have become outcasts because of the cruel soldiers and the cruel *haciendados.* All the time we hide like the animals in the wilderness. We have no homes, no wives and children, no money. Perhaps you have a few of the American dollars you could give us to share with the poor."

"Sell those two horses you stole last night and use the money," Cogin said coldly.

That expansive shrug again. "Ah, no, we need the horses to flee from the cruel ones who oppress us. But with a little money . . ."

Cogin sneered at him. "If you stick around here much longer you won't need money or anything else, sabe? Back over that ridge and down the slope a few miles are a bunch of Apache raiders on my trail. They'll be here any time between now and tomorrow. The best thing you can do is to give us back our horses and get the hell and gone out of here as fast as you can ride. If you don't, you and your men are as good as dead right now."

Lopez laughed at him, leaning back with hands on his slender hips and legs braced apart. "Ho-ho! The American is a very cunning man. You are a liar like all the rest of them. You think to scare Victorio Lopez with these wild stories. You waste your time, mister."

"Have it your own way," Cogin grunted. "But you get no money from us. And if you try to attack us we'll hole up in the rocks and fight it out with you."

"With how much water? What have you in your sacks? How long will it last?"

"Long enough to see you and your two-bit bandits and robbers get cut to pieces by some Apache fighters," was the ominous reply. "I give you one more chance to save your life. Give us back our horses and then get out of here fast."

"Your words are on deaf ears, mister. I am not so much of a fool to believe you. It is the cunning of a North American. I know you well. I have killed two of your prospectors already. They spoke as you speak. So I shall give you one final chance for your lives. We want what money you have, and your guns—"

He broke off, leaving the rest of it unsaid, staring angrily at Cogin's moving back, for Cogin, his patience exhausted quickly, and having something else on his mind, was already returning up the slope down whence he had come. He leaped the narrow chasm again and found Wallace waiting for him, rifle in hand.

"Well?" asked Wallace.

Cogin told him what had happened. Wallace's uneasy face expressed disapproval. "Well, you're crazy, Charley! Why didn't you deal? I've got stacks of money in those two canvas bags, you know. We can buy our way out and buy back our horses. Go down and deal with him."

Cogin reached for the new tobacco sack Wallace had given him to replace his other soaked by the rain. He looked at Wallace and actually grinned. It was a dour expression unusual to his countenance, for he very rarely smiled. He grinned again as the shot spanged out from somewhere down below and a bullet spat off a rock four feet above their heads.

"He wouldn't sell us those cayuses for pure gold because they're too valuable up here, and we couldn't do anything without them. And I deliberately told him about Nino, knowing he wouldn't believe it. So all we have to do is just hole up here in comfort with enough water, and hope that Mr. Lopez won't go away. His shots will tell Nino where to come, and in the melee we just *might* get out of here alive."

Another shot screamed off a rock, but Cogin knew they wouldn't be throwing up too many from down there. Ammunition was too precious. Wallace sat down, grounding the butt of the Spencer between his knees, holding it upright.

"And the others down below?" he asked.

Cogin said coldly, "I've done the best I could for the four. I came after you to get you and take you back down there to help us all, but things kind of came out differently. We're hemmed in by Mexican bandits holding us here for Nino until he comes. So from now on I'm looking out for a man named Charles Cogin and nobody else. We'll fight it out together and try to get away. If we make it and get into the clear, I'll kill you the moment I get a chance."

"So will I," Wallace answered. "Well, now that that's settled, how about you taking that long range gun of yours and burning a few cotton shirt tails?"

"Don't be a damned fool, Wallace. I'm saving ammunition and saving all of them for Nino and his warriors. Just get back up on top and keep an eye open. They think they've got plenty of time, and we haven't got any water. They don't know how little time they have left."

"And neither do we," Wallace the murderer said.

He climbed up into a snug pocket among the rocks above and settled himself with a grunt, cursing silently and bitterly the fates that had brought him to this. It was one thing to go in with a couple of Negro deputies and bring out his men dead or alive, or be packed out himself. It was quite another thing to be hemmed in, helpless to escape.

"Hey, Charley!" he called out suddenly.

"Yeah?" came from below.

"Those birds have probably got poor guns. Why can't we go out of here on foot and you hold them off at long range?"

"Too much timber for them to get close, ride around in front and ambush us, a half-dozen other things. I had that in mind all along. If things get too hot we might try it."

Wallace cursed again and paid no heed to the slug of lead that chipped a white splotch in a rock four feet away. He flattened out on his stomach and eyed the terrain to the west.

Chapter 14

ON THAT same morning, when daybreak showed that the rains had gone and the sun would soon be out to begin drying up the vast land, Nino the raider had already finished breakfast. It had been a particularly good breakfast because some of it had come from the pack on Cogin's dead horse, plus several choice chunks of meat cut from the killed animal's loins. The Apaches had borne the elements of the previous night stoically, but the warmth of the fires was welcome. They were three hundred yards to the south of where the three men and woman were camped.

Some of the younger, more impatient warriors had been grumbling. And so had one or two of the older ones. The brother of the army scout Tacana said it.

"I want the woman," he told Nino. "All my life I have been a good fighter and provider of food for the old and the crippled and my own family as well, but I have never yet burned a woman with long yellow hair. I want to hang her by her heels and let her hair trail down and then watch the fire go through it. All my life I have wanted this thing, and now you say wait."

"We will wait," Nino told him. He was aware of the eyes of the others upon him, saw the sullenness in them at the delay.

"But why must we wait?" argued the older one. "They sit there like sheep, with good horses and many goods. We could have crawled up in the night and taken them all alive. If I were chief . . ."

"You are not a chief as an old man and I am a chief

as a young man," Nino said coldly, the insult at the other's limited abilities plain in his voice. "You know that we cannot attack at night when it can be avoided. The ghosts of the old ones have come down from the abode to roam the desert and sit at our fires and listen to us talk, and they are at peace now. They cannot be disturbed by fighting. These things you know."

He got up and picked up the prized field glasses and made his way to the top of the low ridge that concealed them from the four over there three hundred yards to the north. The Grumbler and one or two of the others followed. Unmindful of the icy cold against his naked belly, Nino lay down in the wet grass and focused the powerful glasses. He saw that the camp had come astir. The picketed horses close by appeared to be well fed and rested. The three foolish White Eyes men were hurriedly preparing something to eat while the foolish woman was at the spring a short distance away, concealed from the others by some rocks. She was changing into a clean dry shirt, her long hair down in back to her hips.

Nino paid no attention to her figure or to the clothes she wore. His eyes were on her hair, that she presently began to comb and then braid. The Grumbler was right. It would make a beautiful flash of fire when strung out below her hanging head.

"Why don't we attack now?" demanded the Grumbler. "Why . . . I could slip over and grab her right now while the rest of the warriors swarmed over the others and captured them all. It would be easy."

Had there been any curse words in the Apache vocabulary Nino most likely would have used them that morning. There being none, then the next best thing was to hurl insults. And the biggest insult of all was to call a man a child. Nino did.

"You are a child," he grunted sneeringly. "You talk like an Apache boy instead of a warrior. Were your eyes not dim with age you could see that Poco's horse is still with them. And does Poco walk off on foot and leave them? Where do you suppose he is?"

"I do not know and care less," came the angry reply. "I only want to burn the woman."

"Poco is an Apache," Nino explained patiently but with a touch of exasperation. "He knew we would follow the party, because he once was one of us and knows how we think and fight. And now he is not with the others because he is up there somewhere in the brush watching and waiting for us to do just what you ask to do. You saw what he did with the big rifle. He killed three of our warriors and wounded another. And now you would go in and let him shoot us all down like rabbits. I will attack when the time is right, and you can burn the woman. But I want Poco more than the others because he is my enemy and will die strong. I will go back and beat my squaw and tell her how I caught him."

He rose to his feet and went back down through the wet grass. The warriors around the small fires said nothing. One of them lay on one of Cogin's blankets, a dirty bandage around the wound in his arm.

The same shot that had killed one of the warriors had gone on through and had cut a furrow in the arm, painful but not serious.

Nino squatted down to warm the cold nakedness of his wet belly, the glow of the bright coals feeling good. He was waiting with the patience and cunning that had made him a chief over much older and more experienced warriors, sending out his thought spirits in an effort to find a good omen.

Over at the fire, however, there was much more activity. The woman Gert came back from the spring. Her grey shirt was dry and clean and the two long braids of hair had been wound about her head in such a manner as not to interfere with the hat she customarily wore. She was hatless now, her face freshly scrubbed; and despite the boots and riding skirt she was an amazingly attractive-looking woman with her tall, square-shouldered figure and rounded bosom.

One-Card, working at his pack, noticed it promptly. In contrast to her his whiskers were scraggly, his clothes dirty and dank-smelling from the rain. He looked more seedy than ever.

"Gert, you look positively beautiful this fine morning," he exclaimed. "I never noticed it until now, really."

"You certainly picked a fine time to," she retorted. "It's not a fine morning, I'm not beautiful, and flattery will get you nowhere with me, One-Card. There never was but one man in the world who meant anything to me, and he's dead. And right now all I'm interested in is getting out of this mess with a live and whole skin and never mind Wallace's money. He can have it all. I did a lot of hard thinking during the night while I was on guard in the cold, and all of a sudden money somehow didn't mean as much as it did in the past."

"Well, it does to me," Bart grumbled. He too was a dank-smelling, dirty sight. "As long as we've come this far and have to fight for our lives, I might just as well fight for Wallace's money."

Hornbuckle said, "Let's have less talk and a little more action. That shot we heard up above might not have been fired by Cogin. It might have been an Apache bullet that *killed* him. But we're here and can't turn back. I haven't seen a thing, but I know they're out there around us somewhere. Maybe straight up the slope. Let's pack up and get out of here pronto. Bart, you saddle Cogin's horse and lead it. One-Card, you'll lead the pack stuff. Gert will ride in front of you a few feet, because she's a good shot with a rifle. I'll bring up the rear a few feet behind. If we get caught, kill the spare horses quick and use them for barricades."

"And," added the woman with a soft smile foreign to her usual demeanor, "when the sun comes up you better take a few good long looks at it. It's a beautiful sight when there's a chance you may never see it rise again."

They finished their chores hurriedly and swung into wet leather. The tracks of the horses dug in deep in the wet ground as the four of them, in a closely packed group, got under way, rifles across their saddles. There was little conversation; little need for it; and certainly little desire for it. They kept to the open as much as possible, working in through clearings. The woman watched ahead to the east; One-Card, with the packhorses' lead ropes tied hard to the saddle horn, watched the north from his side. Beside him, leading Cogin's saddled horse, Bart watched to the south. Bringing up the rear, Hornbuckle rode with his body turned in the saddle, eyes scanning the terrain below to the west.

The sun finally did come out as they climbed higher. So far all was quiet. They saw nothing but were not deceived. They knew that Nino was out there somewhere because Cogin had said so. And in the mind of the woman that made it so. She smiled a little at the thought. He was a cold devil, this Cogin, but he had a lot in him that her late husband had had; he was tall and commanding and with the kind of aloofness that made men respect him.

They came out into a clearing where the timber was falling away toward a larger area of grass still further up. She twisted in the saddle and shifted the rifle, wondering again about Nino.

She was unaware that Nino was very close by now, because Cogin's empty saddle said that Cogin was somewhere up ahead on foot and that the others were going to him. Now was the time to strike.

And Nino struck swiftly, savagely.

Chapter 15

THE FIRST indication that the raiders were anywhere near was when the shrill yell came from a point two hundred yards to the south; Nino's signal. An answering yell came from over on the opposite side, and then the whole area became a scene of murderous activity as the dark forms came at them from all directions. One moment there had been nothing; the next there were sixteen or more coming in at a run, screeching and firing.

The horses began to rear and snort and the woman paid no heed. She was working the lever of her rifle, a .44-40, as fast as she could aim. She heard dimly a terrified cry from One-Card, and even in the maelstrom the thought flashed through her mind: He's no good at gambling and no better in a fight. Bart was yelling and firing too, while Hornbuckle, who had been smoking, clamped his pipe stem between his teeth and coolly shot one warrior dead and then killed the horse of another.

"Up ahead!" cried out the woman. "Spur through them!"

They tried it the best they could, the horses needing little urging. That first savage burst of firing had driven off the raiders. One casualty for them and, as far as she could tell, none for their little party of four.

They were running now with the warriors on each side, and a few shots still banged out. She looked over at One-Card as she feverishly thumbed more cartridges into the magazine. The man was running with the pack horses tied up close, his unshaved face a mask of terror. He was doing no shooting at all, having emptied his pistol as fast as he could pull trigger on the self-cocker. He had dropped his rifle in fright the moment the attack started.

And it was just as she glanced at him that the Apache fired the shot from about a hundred yards away. It struck one of the pack horses tied to One-Card's saddle. The horse went berserk with a scream that was almost human and began to buck and lunge. And when it did One-Card's own mount, spooked completely, took the bit in its teeth and began to run . . . straight toward three of the warriors out there.

"Come back here!" roared Hornbuckle between clenched teeth.

"Fall out of the saddle!" screamed the woman. "Let them go."

Whether he heard her or whether he did it on his own, she didn't know. But he made a leap from the saddle and struck heavily on his back, knocking all the wind out of himself. She saw the swiftly speeding ponies come in at a run with those fierce—visaged, dark—bodied figures hunched up in their rawhide saddles. She shot hard and fast from the back of her own running horse as the three swooped in on One-Card, now bending low in the saddles.

She fired her last shot from the rifle and knocked one of them off his horse, a lucky shot but not enough to prevent what happened. The other two, running side by side, swooped down over One-Card, now trying to rise. Dark arms flashed down and each grabbed him by a hand, an easy trick that they had done since childhood. In the face of the fire the horses cut over into a circle and spurred away out of range, with One-Card dragging between them.

They had him alive, and you could tell it by the chorus of gleeful yells that almost burst their throats.

There was nothing to do but spur on. They came out into the wider clearing now, some six or eight hundred yards across, and saw a cluster of big rocks many feet high. Still in the lead, the woman Gert made straight for the cluster. The Apaches were closing in again for a second raid in the open, trying to cut them off from the sanctuary of the rocks. But fate had intended otherwise that morning.

She heard the booming roar of a heavy rifle up ahead, followed by the crack of a different-toned weapon. The second weapon was being worked with amazing rapidity. The raiders wheeled off from this new and unexpected fire, and the woman Gert spotted the two men up there.

She saw Cogin and she saw Wallace; she caught a startled glimpse of straw sombreros and white cotton shirts and pants fleeing; she saw one of them—*El Señor* Victorio Lopez, the bandit—running straight toward the rock cluster itself.

Then they were around the rocks into a clutter of more rocks and a tarp shelter and the ashes of a cooking fire.

They jerked their panting horses to a halt, saddle leather creaking wetly and nostrils flaring from the hard run as Cogin slid down from above. He was methodically loading his big single-shot .45-70 rifle.

He said, "Well, I see that you made it," and spoke to nobody in particular.

She swung to the ground and pushed up at a hat brim that wasn't there. The wind had carried it away. The sun now shone brightly on the golden braids coiled around her head.

"You didn't come back to us," she explained simply, though no explanation was needed. "So we came to you."

He shrugged. "One place is as good as another. Where's the other fellow?"

"One-Card? The fool had the pack horses tied hard to his saddle horn instead of looping or dallying. When a bullet struck one of them and it went loco, he couldn't get loose, not with his own horse spooked and running with the bit in its mouth. He rode right square into three of them. I got one of them with a lucky rifle shot, but they got him. They got him alive, Cogin," she added with a shudder.

The others had also dismounted and now stood in a small group, huddled up as though for protection. Wallace sat up some ten or twelve feet above them. He was looking down sardonically, though when he looked at the woman with the golden hair, now lit up by the bright sun, the expression in his eyes changed. He was thinking, if she had looked that beautiful down in the settlement when she was after my money, she would have got it and we wouldnt be here like this now. If Cogin can only get us out of this and I can kill him, I'll take her right back, as I should have done at first.

His thoughts were interrupted as he suddenly swung up the Spencer and lined the barrel down at a slant, over the heads of the group below.

"Hold on, you yellow-bellied coyote," he snapped from back of the sights to *El Señor* Victorio Lopez who was panting toward them. "That's close enough."

Lopez stopped and grinned up at him. "Ah, greetings to you, *señor*. My men are the big cowards I have always known they were. But not Lopez. So I come to help you fight the Indios because I'm a very brave man."

"I don't savvy a word you're saying, Bosco, but you got about two seconds to get going before I put a slug between your narrow eyes, you horse-stealing—"

"Hold it, Wallace," Cogin called up. "He came to join us when his men fled."

"He was up within a hundred yards on foot, watching us, and couldn't get away," snarled Wallace. "I could have shot him half a dozen times. I'm going to do it now."

"We'll need his gun," was the reply. And in Spanish to the grinning bandit, "You can come in and fight with us, because we are all now in the same fix. I warned you about the Apaches, but you, *tonto sabia* (wise fool), wouldn't listen."

The mocking smile was still there as Lopez swept off his huge straw sombrero and bowed. "I was the wise fool indeed. And now I offer you my life."

Cogin said to the others, "He's in with us, and maybe that foreign rifle he's carrying will come in handy. But watch him. He'll grab a horse and slip out if he gets half a chance."

The bandit came up among them, and again the sweeping bow, this time to the woman. "Ah, such a beautiful woman for these poor eyes. Now if I die I can die happy, after seeing such beauty."

She asked curiously, "What did he say? My packers talk English."

"Nothing important," grunted Cogin. Hornbuckle was reloading his long-stemmed corncob pipe. He looked at Cogin. "What will they do next, Charley?"

A shrug. "All depends on what Nino thinks. If he can hold us here he'll take his time. If he thinks we might make a break for it tonight, he'll drop the horses from cover."

"And One-Card?"

Again the shrug. "If Nino thinks he has plenty of time with us, he'll stake him out or tie him to a tree. If he thinks we'll try to run for it tonight, he'll either burn him head down today or put him in an anthill."

"Merciful heavens!" shuddered the woman, and there was none of the former hardness in her now. She was a mere woman with a woman's gentle feelings.

"He took his chance," Cogin snapped at her. "He knew what he might run into. He was a gambler and he lost."

"Yes," she nodded slowly. "He was a gambler who lost all his life. And when he made a final big gamble, the biggest of his unfortunate life, he lost that one too."

He didn't answer that one but turned to the others. "There's not room in here for the horses. Take them out a few feet and tie them so that we can make a run for it fast if we get a chance. Hey, Wallace. See anything?"

"Yeah. I see lots of things. They're out there in plain sight but out of range. Just seem to be waiting. They've got the gambling gent tied on the ground but don't seem to be doing anything. Better come up and have a look, Charley. You know more about these mean devils than I do."

He picked up his rifle and started to climb up and found the woman just behind. He reached the top, gave her a hand, and they went over to where Wallace sat peering over the top.

"Maybe they chased them bandits and we could get through what's left," Wallace suggested.

"Not when they've surrounded such a precious quarry as us. They'll kill Mexicans out of habit because they're natural enemies. But we're what he wants . . . and me in particular. We've been enemies for a long time, and an Apache—particularly one like Nino—doesn't forget."

He lay there between the man who had killed his sister and the woman who had hated him because of his indifference but did not any more. Out there he saw them lounging around in groups of twos and threes. In between, alone, were the younger warriors, making a complete circle all around them; ready and waiting for whatever Nino decreed.

"I see they're building a fire over there, but not where

One-Card is bound, thank heaven," the woman's voice beside him said. "Looks like they feel pretty confident of us to sit down and eat in the middle of the morning."

He said, "Go over and tell one of the men below to build up a fire and then have some green brush ready. Nino will be wanting to talk."

She shot him that strange look that sometimes came across her face, now within inches of his own, but obeyed. Minutes passed. None of the warriors had moved. Some sat their horses as immobile as stone statues. Others lounged on the ground near their ponies. Hornbuckle and the others were on guard down below. Presently a plume of smoke arose out there in the distance, and with it came the distant boom of a big rifle. A leaden slug struck into the rocks, fired from long distance, and went off into the sky with a wheezing scream.

"Oh, oh!" ejaculated Wallace. "So he wants to talk, eh? —like that."

"He'll want to talk in person, and that was just to let me know that all his men are not armed with old guns. He's just warning me that if I try anything funny, that apache gunner of his will know what to do."

The first puff balls began to go up, and Cogin lay there and watched them as of old, thinking that had it not been for that shot through his shoulder those years before at the settlement—the shot that had taken him from the Apaches and returned him to the whites—then most likely he himself would be out there with Nino or perhaps in Nino's place.

There was a brief interval between the puff balls, and then they began again. After that a single, yellowish puff and no more. The message was ended.

Cogin hurriedly slid down the face of the rock to the fire. Hornbuckle had built it and broken off some green branches. From above the tense face of the woman watched as he covered the fire with the evergreens and picked up Wallace's saddle blanket. Not a sound came from the group as he spread the blanket over the smoke and went to work. The answering puff balls rolled straight up out of the huge cluster of rocks and into the breezeless morning sky. The others stood silently and waited as the answer continued to shoot up, their faces expressing various emotions. Finally he tossed the blanket aside and rose.

"What's it all about?" Hornbuckle asked.

"Nino wants to talk with his 'brother.' Says he'll meet me halfway, alone under a white flag. That means a word of honor. I'll go see what he wants."

"Yeah?" asked Bart. "And make a deal to leave us here while you get away?"

"Shut up, Bart," Hornbuckle snapped. And to Cogin! "Think there's any way you could get us free? Maybe the promise of lots of horses or something?"

"He can get all he wants in Mexico and from ranches north of the line. I'll go see what he wants."

He picked up his rifle and went out to the horse Bart had led saddled from the previous camp. He shoved the big weapon into its boot and was preparing to swing up when he felt a hand on his shoulder; a hand so gentle it was almost timid. He let his foot down out of the stirrup and faced her.

"Charley, I'm scared," she said pleadingly.

"So am I," he said harshly.

"You're the only hope we have to get out of here alive."

"I didn't ask you to come," he told her in that quiet, hard way that years among his family had never been able to soften. It was the remnants of the Apache in him. He was talking—and thinking—like an Apache now.

She nodded humbly. "I know you hate me because I was greedy, because it's been suspected that I killed my husband. But I don't want to fall into the hands of those cruel things out there. If anything happens that you don't come back, what must we do?"

He looked at her out of blue eyes that were without emotion. "Keep shooting until you have one bullet left. Then use it."

He swung up into the seat, reined the horse around,

and rode out from the cluster of rocks. He saw another figure on a horse, over there in the edge of the timber to the south, gig into motion and ride out to meet him halfway.

After twelve years he and Nino were to meet again . . . still enemies.

Chapter 16

THEY JOGGED on toward each other while the eyes of those hemmed in the rock cluster and the eyes of the stoically waiting warriors watched. The pony bearing Nino came on, slowed to a walk, and Cogin looked him over.

He hasn't changed much, he thought. He's a little taller now and matured, but his face is the same, and I know he saw me through those glasses of Hornbuckle's and was grinning when he called by smoke for a talk.

The ponies were within thirty feet of each other when both riders came to a halt. Nino was naked to the waist and wore a rag around his forehead but did not have the lateral streak of white beneath his eyes. He might have washed it off before riding out. At any rate they sat there for a few minutes and stared at each other without speaking, as was customary. Nino carried a Henry rifle across his saddle; a thirteen-shot weapon used very successfully during the Civil War but, like the big Spencer, not much for long range. Finally he gigged his tough little pony into a walk and they came up close. Cogin still waited in silence. It was Nino who spoke.

"So Poco has come back to the land of the Apaches and the Me-hi-canos?"

"I have returned to the land of the Americanos and the

Me-hi-canos. The Apaches have no lands now. The White Eyes have taken it from you."

Nino's eyes flashed, but he said nothing as he swung down from his pony and Cogin followed suit. By common action they sat down on their haunches, facing each other, studying each other in detail.

"It is good to see you again after all these years, but you are a White Eyes now and my enemy."

"That is true."

"There are many things of the old days we could talk about."

"Many things. I remember the old ones, the warriors, the pretty girls like Keneta."

Nino's eyes flashed with a touch of boastfulness back of a plain grin. "She is my squaw now and in my *jacal* with three little ones," holding up three fingers.

"She would be mine to beat now if you had pulled me off the ground the morning of the big raid when I was taken by the White Eyes. But you were young and weak then and could not lift me."

"I was never young and weak. I have been strong all my life. I have been a chief for six grasses now."

This was the kind of preliminary thing that had to be done before Nino stated his purpose in calling for a talk. They spent several minutes talking over their boyhood days together: the summer hunting trips, their training by the older warriors, the various fights. Cogin did not ask about those who might now be dead. Once a warrior was gone to the abode, his name was never mentioned again. They discussed the recent raids and Nino did a bit of boasting about how the White Eyes soldiers could not get him, even with scouts like old Tacana helping them.

This brought the opening that Cogin had been waiting for. He said, "I saw Tacana with the White Eyes soldiers a few suns back."

"His brother, the Grumbler, is with us now."

"And does he, too, hate the White Eyes you now have surrounded in the rocks?"

"He wants to burn the woman with the yellow hair

and watch the fire go through it. I have one of your warriors as a prisoner. But he will not die strong. I have come to trade you this weak one for the woman with the yellow hair."

He was very sincere about it, because to him a squaw was something to work hard, bear children, and be beaten at her husband's will. He appeared genuinely surprised when Cogin refused. He grunted his contempt—and perhaps disappointment.

"The White Eyes have made you weak and foolish, Poco. You are no longer an Apache. But you will die strong, and I will go back and beat Keneta and tell her how you died."

It was Cogin's turn to grunt his contempt. "Two suns back I killed three of your warriors and wounded another. Alone. You were many and I was one. I killed your warriors and escaped. Now I have White Eyes with good guns and I have one Me-hi-cano with a good gun. You are a fool."

Nino's smoldering black eyes flashed and his lips thinned. No man yet had ever called him a fool and lived.

"You have no water except in your skin bags. None for your horses. I have much water and much time. My warriors will dump much water on the ground for you to see while the sun burns your tongue."

"Warriors cannot dump water without eyes to see. They will have no eyes by the time the sun burns my tongue." (This was in reference to the fact that certain birds such as magpies always got to a dead man before the coyotes and buzzards and pecked out the eyes. It also was another insult to Nino.)

It made him angry. That was plain to see in his burning eyes and the way his mouth had lost its grin and was now a thin, twisted slit set in his almost black face. But he patiently tried another tack, the first having failed.

"You are a White Eyes now, but were a great warrior even when young and fighting with your people. You belong with us again because, no matter how many White

Eyes soldiers we kill, more come like the leaves of grass to take their places. Our numbers are few and we do not have others to replace the ones gone to the abode. You have lived among the White Eyes for many grasses now. Twelve grasses," holding up all fingers and thumbs and then two more. "You know their ways. Bring the woman with you and come with us and I will let the others live. Take the woman as your squaw and fight with us until they give us peace. Then you can talk for us and be a great man."

It didn't sound, on the surface, as illogical as it might have under other circumstances. Cogin could have done that very thing. That would have freed the others, saved himself along with the woman, and he might have been able to make the higher chiefs realize just how hopeless their fight against the whites was. Some of them had never wanted to fight and, for that matter, still didn't. A few of the tough, treacherous ones like Geronimo did.

Cogin shook his head. "I am not a fool and I do not listen to a warrior who speaks with a forked tongue."

"I speak with a straight tongue," snapped Nino, rising to his feet, the muzzle of the gun held so carelessly but slanting dangerously close toward Cogin's waist.

"You broke your word to the White Eyes soldiers many times. You said you would raid no more. Now you would take me to your camp and burn the woman's hair and tie me to a post and work on me as you helped work on the soldier when we were together, when you dropped the live coal on top of his head after three days at the post. You would capture the others in the rocks and do the same. Then you would return to your band and boast. We will speak no more."

He too had risen and stood beside his horse. They both mounted cautiously. Nino sat eyeing him warily, the anger and disappointment plain in his eyes. Both his bluff and his trickery had failed.

He said, "We will speak no more until I have you at the post. Then I will talk with you for three days because you will die strong."

He turned his back and rode away, and Cogin did the same. Up in the rocks Wallace, flat beside the woman, heaved a sigh of relief. He had told her the circumstances of Cogin and himself being in camp together, and now he spoke again.

"I don't know what happened out there, Gert. We'll know pretty soon now. But I've just finished telling you what's going to happen if we get free. One of us has got to kill the other. I think it'll be me. That means you and I can take my money and start out new some place where we're not known . . . and I've got plenty of money. Two whole canvas sacks of it down there under the tarp. It's yours for the asking."

Her eyes were still on Cogin, now loping toward the place where the others waited so anxiously. She said, "I've had many men try to buy me, but none under quite such circumstances. We're not out of this yet by a long shot. You'd better guard your money and keep your rifle handy. I'm going down and see what happened."

Chapter 17

COGIN CAME back and swung from his horse. The anxious eyes of the group were upon him. He strode in among the rocks, rifle in hand.

"Any luck?" asked Hornbuckle in a voice studiously casual.

"About what I expected," Cogin replied. "He tried bluff and then trickery."

"What kind of bluff and trickery?"

"He wanted to trade One-Card for the woman so they

can burn her yellow hair. He thought quite honestly that he was offering a good bargain. To them a woman means little except a creature to work and be beaten, but One-Card handling a rifle against them was his idea of giving us the best of the deal. I didn't bother to tell him that the woman here can handle a gun more effectively than One-Card. So when I turned him down he made an offer that sounded really good. He said that the rest of you could go scot-free if I'd bring the woman as my squaw and come back and join the tribe for a while as an adviser until peace is made. Said I'd be very valuable in talking terms with the soldiers because I've lived among the whites for so long."

"That don't sound like trickery to me," broke in Bart excitedly, hitching at the belt below his protruding stomach. "That sounds like good common sense. We could all get out of here with whole skins, even old One-Card. You ain't goin' to let 'em torture One-Card and the rest of us, are you?"

The woman said, "You think it's trickery, Charley? I'd go with you in a minute if you said it was all right. If you want a 'squaw,' say the word."

"Thanks," Cogin said dryly. "But it's not all right. They'd burn you, bury One-Card in an anthill, and put me to a post for three days. The rest of you wouldn't have a chance."

"But you know them people!" Bart cried out again.

Cogin said coldly, "Yes, I know Nino. That's why I turned him down."

"Well, what's the next move then?"

"We'll wait, of course. We can't do anything else at the moment."

"Frankly, Cogin, I think that's plain damned foolishnes," Hornbuckle put in. "The longer we stay here the worse shape our horses will be in. If we come out of here with guns going and fight hard enough, some of us at least might get through. And to my mind that's a lot better than winding up in their hands. I'll take my chance."

"So will I!" cried Bart.

"That goes for me too, Charley," Wallace called down.

"What about you?" Cogin asked the woman.

"You're the one man who can get us out of this fix, if anybody can. Without you there's no doubt of what the end will be. I'll do whatever you say."

"Well, well, well!" jeered Bart, and gave off a coarse laugh. "So our hard, tough, treedy Gert, who didn't have nothin' to do with no man, is now a soft woman?" He changed his voice to a shrill simper: " 'If you want a squaw, just say the word, darling. I'll do anything you say, dearie. Just anything a-tall.' "

He turned to Hornbuckle, the small eyes set in his flabby face cold and piercing, determination written in them. "Horn, let's you and me and Wallace take that Mexcan there and the four of us fight our way outa here. Some of us can get through. And if these two moonstruck love birds wanta stay here and gaze up at the—"

Cogin struck just once, swiftly. His right fist smashed hard against the man's jaw, and Bart went down heavily, a loud grunt emanating from his huge chest. He wagged his head from side to side to clear it and rubbed at his hairy jowl. Cogin stood over him.

"You got yourself into this mess with the others. If you hadn't come along—the whole party, I mean—the Apaches would never have caught sight of me; and they couldn't have caught me even if they had seen me. I would have caught and killed Wallace by now—"

"—in an anthill," Wallace couldn't help jeering from above.

"I could have finished the job and been on my way. But you helped get me in here and you're going to help get me out, if it can be done. It's the woman and me Nino particularly wants. He wants to burn that yellow hair of hers and he wants me at a post for three days, because the woman he's married to once turned him down on account of me and hurt his vanity. So we stay. I'll kill the first man, or woman, who tries to pull out of here."

That appeared to settle the matter. Bart got to his

feet, glowering and, for moment, cowed, but the murderous fury in his eyes was plain. Cogin ordered him to go out and loose all the cinches on the saddles and bring back the water sacks and canteens. After that it was a matter of settling down to wait. The sun crawled up higher and the heat struck the rocks and turned the hemmed in group sweaty. Out beyond gunshot range the warriors waited patiently. One-Card, still trussed, had been dragged into the shade of a tree; not because of any compassion on the part of his captors but because they themselves were in the shade and wanted him close.

Cogin divided the group into two watches while the others rested beneath what shade Wallace's rigged up tarp had to offer. The sun reached its zenith, beating down upon the huddled up horses and their huddled up riders. Still the Apaches made no move that indicated action. Nino still lounged in the shade and One-Card still lay trussed up on the ground not far away. When the shade moved away, they let him lie. He had been given no water.

Late that evening the woman crawled up on top and look her place beside Cogin. He lay on his stomach, the big single-shot rifle beside him. It was cooler now and the group had ceased to seat, but not to grumble. On the surface they were sticking together, almost enemies all, but bound of necessity. Only the Mexican Lopez still appeared to be cheerful. He never lost his mocking grin, bravado though it might have been. It was possible that, being the only Mexican among them, he wanted to show these *Norteamericanos* that his brand of courage was superior to theirs. He could talk a little with Hornbuckle, who spoke some Spanish, and told many boasting tales of his outlaw exploits. And once, when a warrior rode in a little too close, the Mexican threw a long range shot at him with the foreign-made rifle that threw up a puff of dust beside the pony and sent its rider scuttling back out of range.

The woman Gert lay down beside Cogin. She said, "They're certainly in no hurry, are they, Charley?"

He turned and looked at her in that hard, blunt way of

his. "Nino has plenty of time. He might try something after dark. They don't like to, because during the night the peaceful ghosts of their departed ones come down from the abode and sit around their fires to listen to them talk. Right now Nino is sending his thought spirits at me."

She gave him a startled look. "Trying to communicate with you?"

"That's about the size of it," he nodded. "He's gloating at me, telling me what will happen when I'm tied to a post. The Apaches do this with all their enemies in a siege like this. They believe that the thought spirits come through and that it scares their enemies and makes them nervous and destroys their fighting efficiency when the final showdown comes. There's a lot of whites believe it too."

"And you?"

"I'm getting a little nervous, if that's what you mean. And he knows I'm getting nervous. That's why he's sending them at me."

She didn't speak for some time, just lying there beside him with her chin on her crossed forearms. Then:

"Tell me something, Charley. You said Nino hates you because of an Apache girl you took from him. A few days ago I wouldn't have asked you anything like this . . . but that was a few days ago, even years. Things have changed much among us all since then. You, Wallace, myself; poor Limpy and poor One-Card lying out there in the sun all day. But about the girl—"

He said, his eyes out on the distant panorama of the great Sierre Madre, "Her name was Keneta and we'd all been just a bunch of Apache kids playing and growing up together. But when she was fourteen she went through her puberty rites, lasting for three days of praying and dancing and other ceremonies. After that she was a woman and eligible for marriage. I was just turning sixteen and so was Nino. So he put his horses in front of her *jacal* one night and let them stay tied there all the next day, which was customary. But when, on the second day, she didn't come out and lead them to water, Nino had to come get them and lead them off again. His suit had been rejected. Nino and me hadn't been exactly good friends anyhow, and when she threw a stick at me a day or two later . . . well, that turned us into bitter enemies."

"Would you have married her?" she asked.

His eyes were still gazing out there in the distance, watching everything that moved. He said, "After the Apaches come back from a big raid they always pull a celebration of feasting and dancing and any marriage rites in the offing. My marriage rites to Keneta were coming up when we made the big raid on the settlement and I got shot off my horse. That was the morning when I'd just shot Limpy's leg almost in two. Nino ran by on his horse and made a grab at my hand like those two warriors got One-Card, but he missed. If it hadn't been for his grasp slipping on my hand that morning, I'd be married to Keneta by now and maybe out there in his place this morning instead of in here."

She actually smiled at him. "And I suppose you'd burn my hair over a fire while I hung by my heels from a cottonwood limb?"

"Yes," he said slowly. "It would have been a beautiful sight, watching the fire go through it and listening to you—"

"Stop it!" she broke in with a shudder. "It's too horrible to think of."

It was his turn to smile at her. "I wouldn't have thought so had I remained as one of them. They know nothing else. It's been their way of life, all the tribes, for a hundred generations before the first whites came over from England and settled on the east coast."

Chapter 18

THE SUN moved on down toward the western horizon and the shadows began to lengthen. Far, far below, miles away through openings in the trees, they could see the desert, its broad expanse turning color. The buzzards that had been circling all day as though in anticipation of what was to come now turned lazily on outspread wings and moved on down to the canyons toward their caves; hundreds of them in many flights. The men not on guard were preparing supper from one of the packs. Cogin still remained above the woman beside him. Neither had moved or spoken for some time. He was busy with thoughts of the coming night, of Wallace who would kill him at the first opportunity, of what he would do if he should get out alive.

There was nothing in Kansas to go back to. It was gone, put behind him, something to be forgotten. There was nothing particular in store for him ahead. He thought of the shooting star he had seen that night as he lay on his tarp back of Limpy's corral in the little settlement from whence they all, except the Mexican, had come. And he thought of the night ahead as darkness came down.

She lay beside him and watched as the horizon moved in closer around them, a dark circle drawing in tighter and tighter on their vision, shortening it until it soon would be but a few feet in circumference. Out there a pin-point of light lit up and she watched it, saw the lamp with its smoky globe. He must have gone to sleep and the wick flared up. . . .

He stirred as she came into the room, and opened his

eyes. She heard his groan again as she had heard it day and night for two weeks. She saw the blood on his lips when he spat feebly. He didn't look much like the tall, suave, soft-spoken man who had first seen her in the store that day in Texas; clean-shaven, immaculately dressed, a gentleman all the way through. Neither did the hands that had caressed her, later held her tight against him, and—still later—taught her how to handle a deck of cards over a dealer's chair. "Tall Jim" Saunders, the gambler.

That you, hon?

Of course it is.

Did you get it?

Darling, I told you there is none in this tough tent mining camp. There's no drug store, not even a doctor here.

Then go get my six-shooter from where you've hidden it. Hon, this pain . . . I can't stand it any more.

You'll have to stand it. You'll get well. I know it.

He had laughed his hollow laugh again and spat more red colored spittle.

Sure, I'll get well. With my lungs eaten up by something that causes blood to come up. Did you ever see a man dying with a bullet in his lungs, see the terrible pain he goes through? I have. Many times. That's what's in my lungs. No one bullet but a hundred that are biting away like red hot pokers. Hon, please . . . get me my gun and then just walk out and leave me. I can't stand it.

She had sat on the cot beside him in the big tent, pitched high in an Arizona gulch, on a hillside. The lamp was still smoky. She let it smoke as she reached into the pocket of her dress and brought out the bottle of laudanum. Tincture of Opium, it said on the label, and she'd lied to him and said there was none to be had in camp.

His eyes were closed in pain when she kissed him on the forehead and quietly left the tent. At the flap she turned. The lamp globe she had cleaned now lit up the tent brightly.

On the table beside it, within reach of his frail hand, stood the bottle that would ease his pain . . . forever.

The miners' drumhead court had been pretty tough about it, after word got around that she'd been trying to buy some laudanum. Tall Jim had been a square gambler who never cheated, who'd hand back part of his winnings to a miner in need of a stake, who never turned a deaf ear to a hungry man.

The verdict: We, the jury find you guilty of killin' yer sick husband, Tall Jim Saunders, him comin' to his death by an overdose of laudanum you give him on purpose to git him outa the way so's maybe you kin have a freer hand with some of the gents who's allus around yer table. We ain't hangin' no woman, but now that Tall Jim is under the sod in his last restin' place, you are herewith banished frum this yer camp now an' forever. An' we'll spread the word all over this yer territory, so's folks will know you for whut you are. You got anything to say before you turn yer back in this yer camp?

I have plenty to say. This 'trial' was a masterpiece of self-righteousness and stupidity as only narrow and ignorant men could hold one. There was no well meant justice. I'm not rurning my back to you. I'm turning my face—at bay. Somewhere, somehow, I'm going to find a stake. When I make it I'm going to put up the biggest gambling hall in the newest and biggest boom camp in Arizona, where I'll meet all of you again. And when I do I'll render a verdict of my own. I'll take every penny that you dig out of the ground and send you on your way, broke and dirty, like the uncouth, ignorant tramps that you are.

Later, when she had had time to think more coherently, she had regretted the outburst, but that had not lessened her determination. Smuggling had been the way out, a means of making a stake and deliberately encasing herself in a hard shell that no man could penetrate to touch her sympathy and affections. But her notoriety had spread far and wide and too many saloon owners bought their goods elsewhere. She had fought it out doggedly, still hoping for the stake that had not materialized.

Not until a man named Wallace had come along.

Wallace the gun fighter, and he had what she needed: His money and his guns. . . .

There were more fires springing up out there now, a full circle all around them. Gertrude Saunders still lay silently beside Cogin. Now she stirred and sat up.

"The others have eaten. I'll send Wallace up to relieve you."

The night wore on as they all finished eating and cleaned up camp. Wallace was up on top on one side and Hornbuckle on the other. All was quiet. Bart was asleep beneath the tarp, snoring loudly. Cogin, the woman, and the Mexican Lopez sat in the light of the fire. The Mexican was still his same cheerful self. He jerked a thumb toward the tarp.

"He makes more noise than the steam train, I think," he grinned at Cogin, who interpreted. "One of my men who run away, all the time he snore until one night I get up and hit him over the head with a stick. After that he don't snore no more."

He rose, went out to the horses, and worked through them, hands on their necks, came back again, shaking his head.

"We've got to get some water for them some way," he said, the grin for once gone. "It was hot all day and they had no water. Tomorrow will be worse."

Gertrude Saunders stirred on her seat, a rock by the fire. "Tell me something, Charley. Why couldn't we make a break for it in the darkness when they can't see to shoot?"

"We could try it except for one reason," he said. "I'm not exactly squeamish after the way things shaped up my life for me. Maybe it's just because things have changed a little lately. I can't go until I make a try for One-Card. After all, he's a white man."

"I knew it!" she exclaimed softly. "I knew it. You, the cold, hard man without emotion, caring nothing for anybody on this earth. But you're risking your life—all our lives—to keep him from getting tortured."

"Hey," called Wallace's voice softy from above, "better

come up and have a look, Charley. There's something going on out there not too far away."

Cogin climbed back up, peering over. There was something about two hundred yards away, or even closer. He could hear a few muffled sounds that were too indistinct to clarify. Not likely they would try to fire the grass. The ground was still damp and there was no wind.

"They don't make noise like that when they're coming in," he said to the gun fighter. "You don't hear a thing. They—"

Commotion came from below, among the horses. There was the slap of a body hitting leather, the grunt of a horse as spurs dug in, and then the animal went smashing away down the slope as hard as it could go.

"Cogin, it's the Mexican!" cried out the woman. "He's gone!"

The horse was running fast; that could be told by the sounds of its hoofs. Bart had come alive and, thinking quickly for once in his life, leaped toward the tied horses to prevent a spook. Lopez was driving it hard for a point between two of those distant fires, which appeared to be about one hundred and fifty yards apart in the circle.

"The dirty stinking scum!" swore Wallace angrily. "And you're the gent who wouldn't let me shoot him when I saw the chance. Well," he added grimly, "maybe he had the right idea instead of yourn. And I'll bet you ten to one of my stolen bank money that he makes it."

"I'll just take that bet," Cogin grunted back. "They're not out there at those fires except to keep them burning. They're laying in close and quiet to see what we're doing. About a hundred yards—"

He didn't get to finish it before he had won the bet. Just about one hundred yards away there came a flash of fire, a tiny pin-point accompanied by a booming roar in the night. It was slanted up as though from a man standing on the ground, and it was within ten feet of the running horse. There came a scream, the thud of a body hitting the ground, and then the boom of another gun, this time the flame pointing down at a slant toward the ground.

"Pay me," said Cogin grimly. "He rode right between two of them, lying out there on their bellies and maybe hoping to crawl in and get at the horses. Nino would like that. Bart," he called down, "you stay with those horses every minute—and don't get any ideas."

"Not me," grunted an answer from below. "If I had any like him, I ain't got 'em any more."

From the night all around them came the shrill barking of coyotes. It went on for at least two minutes and then ceased; changed to shrieks of laughter and shrill, gleeful yells. All the way around them. Presently all was quiet again.

All except for those strange sounds coming from out there about two hundred yards away.

Chapter 19

COGIN TURNED to Wallace, the man who had killed his sister and whom he'd trailed so many hundred miles. He shifted the newly filled belt of .45-70's to a more comfortable position over his shoulder. He still wore his moccasins.

"I'm going out and do a little scouting. I want to see what's going on out there."

"You got any idea?"

"Yes," was the reply. "I'm beginning to get an idea." He made no further explanation. "You keep your eyes open and all your guns within reach. If anything breaks loose out there, shoot at anything that moves this way until you hear me whistle twice. I'll be close up, and you can hear me plainly. It'll mean that I'm coming in. And you'd better keep an eye on Bart. If I get into a ruckus over there to the south, he might try to break through on the north. And give me that long sheath knife you're packing."

Wallace complied in silence and Cogin slid down the rock. Hornbuckle had come down for a moment and was smoking his pipe. Cogin told him the same as he had told Wallace. The little man nodded thoughtfully. He didn't ask any questions. He was one of the party who had never let his thoughts turn back upon his past life. They were locked up in one of the dark caverns of his mind, sealed off forever.

"Two whistles," he said. "I'll remember and tell Gert up above. And don't worry—I'll keep an eye on Bart."

Cogin nodded and tossed his hat onto a nearby rock. Hats made an outline in the night to a man lying flat on his stomach. He moved past the horses and faded like a shadow as Hornbuckle climbed up beside the woman. Once they thought they heard a rock rattle somewhere down below and close by, but that was all.

The night had swallowed him into its black maw.

He worked his way southward on his stomach, placing the rifle out at arm's length ahead and then pulling himself up to it. Three pulls forward and then a brief pause to listen. He covered fifty yards and then a hundred. The sounds were coming more distinctly now but no voices, which was to be expected. He heard the distant howls of the coyotes, few among the millions that roamed these ranges with little fear of man. The grass slid by beneath his shirt and cartridge belts, but he made no sound as he moved on steadily toward his objective. He was an Apache now, stalking them in their own way on their own ground.

It took him about forty-five or fifty minutes to reach a point where he could see anything that moved, but he could not as yet tell how many were in the party. He thought: I hope one of them is Nino. If I can just kill him that will be the end of it. They'll fade away in the night and head for the territory and their home grounds.

That was the real reason he had refused to let the party

try to fight its way out of the Apache encirclement. They might have made it . . . some of them. But even so there still would be fifty or sixty miles between them and the nearest Mexican settlement or big hacienda.

But there had been no use to explain this to the others, because he had never been a man to explain things. The four fools had gotten themselves into this mess and had looked to him to get them out. He was trying it now, the Apache way.

About two hundred yards down the slope, to the east, he heard a horse snort and then begin to slobber uneasily; the two warriors who had killed Lopez finally catching up with the saddle horse that now no longer bore a fleeing rider. But Cogin paid it no heed. He was too close now, could see the three-foot-high, cone-shaped mound where the Apaches were working.

Four of them, he thought, and it looks like they've just about got him buried up to the neck. Nino wants him there for me to see in the morning; just his head sticking out of the ground. But there was no use in telling the others. Well, I'm glad I didn't have to use a rifle at two hundred yards.

The four were kneeling and squatting around the head sticking up out of the ground, raking the dirt up close around the neck. Another couple of minutes and they would be gone silently, not even the rustle of the grass telling of their passing. Cogin carefully laid down the Sharps rifle and eased his hand back to his sheath. He removed the six-shooter, having slipped in an extra shell to fill the empty chamber he usually left beneath the hook hammer. Wallace's knife came free of the sheath. It was a long-bladed Bowie and honed to a hair-bladed edge.

He was within six feet of them now, the ant mound between them. With a long intake of breath that told of the tension within, he drew up one leg to a knee position, gathered himself and sprang.

He was almost on top of them before they were aware of his presence, and the .44 in his hand was already lashing fire. He shot the first, the second. He killed the third.

As the fourth sprang toward a rifle Cogin's fourth shot knocked him down into the grass. But the Apache was up in a flash, trying to swing the rifle, his shrill screech splitting the night. Cogin lunged in and swung at him first with his right hand and then with his left.

The gun barrel brought a yell of pain as it struck the warrior's shoulder. The slash of the knife cut it off fast. From out in the night came a series of shrill yells. They had seen the firing, heard the four shots, the yell of warning.

And they were coming. You could hear their ponies drumming hard, their cries. Cogin bent over the four peering into each face and a grunt of disappointment went through him. He had risked all on Nino being present, on ending this thing in one savage attack. Now they were coming, he was afoot, and even if he escaped Nino would know and would not risk another such deadly raid by the White Eyes who had been an Apache.

As for Cogin, there was one small grain of satisfaction in that brief moment as he bent over the last of the four. The man who had been killed with a knife had gone to the abode with his one big ambition in life unfulfilled.

The Grumbler would never burn a woman with blonde hair.

Cogin straightened and leaped for the rifle that he had left a few feet away. He came up and stood there a moment, listening to the sounds around him, spotting their positions, the number of them.

Then he stepped forward and looked down, a fleeting thought going through his mind as to what the others were doing back among the rocks.

What was happening back there was in the hands of Wallace. He had lain up there at his post as Cogin faded away into the night, admiration in him at the cold daring of a man who would go it like that alone. A man he intended to kill if Cogin came back alive. He had no doubt about the outcome, for he was a gun fighter and

Cogin was not. Cogin was the type who killed swiftly, without warning perhaps, and certainly without that tight feeling in the stomach that Wallace always got.

A boot scraped from below and the woman crawled up beside him. It had been fifteen minutes since Cogin had disappeared out there somewhere; fifteen of the longest minutes three men and a woman had ever experienced. She felt herself shivering a little, and Wallace, cold-nerved and calloused man that he was, turned, the darkness hiding the sardonical look on his face.

"Getting worried about him?" he asked.

"Worried? I'm ice all over. This silence and waiting, not knowing what's going on out there or what will happen."

"You'll know pretty soon," he grinned. "I've finally figgered out what that noise is."

"What?"

"Didn't get it for quite a while. Guess I'm dumb, because I've been looking at it all day, aiming my rifle at it and thinkin' it was near the size of an Apache, thinkin' about how Cogin would like to have me out there by it, tied hand and foot."

"What are you talking about?" she demanded.

"An anthill, Gert. A big anthill out there two hundred yards or less. Them sounds weve been hearing are some bucks burying One-Card up to his neck; digging sounds with their knives and throwing axes. Cogin knew it too, Gert. That's why he's out there."

"Why . . . of course," she said softly. "He said he wouldn't leave because of One-Card. And now he's risking everything to get out there and bring him back. He's cold as ice, Wallace. He's hard and brutal like the Apaches who raised him, like this country itself is. But he's risking death and torture to do something none of us would do."

"He might as well," came the grunted reply through the night. "If he gets back and we get out it's going to happen anyhow. Because, Gert, I'm a gunfighter and he's not."

"He's not the kind of a man who kills easily."

"He will be. And when he does go down it'll be you and me with my money. I was a fool not to have taken you up on that deal when I was in the settlement."

He was unaware that her eyes were looking at him from two feet away, something of the old hardness in them, her face harsh and disgusted.

She said coldly, "That was back at the settlement, Wallace, when I was desperate to get out of there; just any way at all. That was before I knew you killed Cogin's younger sister. Oh, yes," she half jeered at him. "I know. When Cogin came in after you he wouldn't talk. We thought he was a bounty hunter, then. That's why we jumped on your trail. Limpy and One-Card and Bart and Horn . . . and me. We became 'bounty hunters' too. Then last night just before Cogin started on up after you on foot to bring you and your guns back to help us, he told us everything. That there was no bounty on your head, that the money would be returned to the banks from which it came, that you had killed his sister. I didn't mention it because this hasn't been the time and place to mention it. But you might as well know. I'd almost rather walk into an Apache camp alone than go with a murdering gun-fighting woman killer like you."

"So you found out?" he sneered back at her. "And now you want Cogin, who's years younger than you."

"I doubt it. I'm twenty-nine. Not that it makes any difference. Cogin is a man with a single purpose, and there is no room in his life for anything else. A strange man who has a lot of qualities that my husband had."

"Well," he sneered at her again, "if I know Cogin, it won't do you any good. The day I dropped by their ranch up in Kansas to rest over for a few days, he didn't even shake hands with me. Just looked at me out of those cold eyes and walked away toward the corrals. His foolish old father was always boasting about his Apache life until I got sick and tired of it. Anyhow, when that little seventeen-year-old kept flirting with me and teasing me and then laughed at me, all I did was to kind of slap the daylights out of her. I didn't intend to hurt her. It was just my temper. So I slapped her, and she squalled and said she was going to tell her brother something awful about me. Well, people don't do that to Bas Wallace. So I hauled my stakes, knowing he'd be on my trail. That's why I wouldn't go with you from the settlement. I wanted to keep driving south deep into Mexico where I could buy protection with Mexican politicos to look out after me when he came. Down there I could have got him at—"

"Listen!" she interrupted.

They listened, but the night brought back only silence and the continual howl of the distant coyotes. It went on that way as the minutes passed. She was ready to go back down when the shots came.

Out there two hundred yards or less from them came the four distinct roars of Cogin's six-shooter and two screeches that were not those of a white man. Wallace lifted his head higher and heard the drumming of hoofs from all over the darkness. He leaped to his feet and grabbed her by the arm.

"Come on quick! They've got him, Gert. We've got to get out of here. He'll never break through."

He jumped down below and she followed him, the fear deep in her that more tragedy was coming. Hornbuckle looked down from above.

"Get back to your post, Wallace," he snapped.

"Post, nothing! I'm getting out of here quick. Cogin's done for, and those warriors on the north side are pounding around to take a hand. We're in the clear!"

He dived for the tarp shelter, fumbled around for a minute, lit a match and fumbled some more. And then his scream of rage filled the night.

"It's gone, it's gone!" he bellowed. "My money in the two canvas sacks. Who took it? Which one of you?"

Hornbuckle looked down from four feet above, and his voice came calmly. "Why, the Mexican, of course, Wallace. None of us would be fools enough. That's why he was hanging around the horses all the time. Well, it looks like Nino is a very rich man now."

Wallace stood there almost panting. The sweat actually broke out on his forehead in the darkness. Bart had run in and was half shouting questions. Hornbuckle slid down, and Wallace stood there cursing with every oath he could think of, the bitter gall making his mouth dry. He had risked his life and killed two men to get that money. He had been trailed hundreds of miles as a fugitive, living in fear of one man catching up with him from behind. And now . . .

He swallowed and calmed down a bit. He said hoarsely, "I'm leaving, and Gert's coming with me. We're breaking through."

Her calm voice said, "Gert is staying right here and not leaving."

"Calm down, Wallace," Hornbuckle said coldly. "We stay."

"We do like hell!"

His hand flashed to his hip and dipped up. He shot Hornbuckle twice and then wheeled on Bart, standing within three feet. Bart never knew what hit him, because the bullet caught him squarely between the eyes.

Wallace wheeled on her. "Now, damn you," he panted. "Cogin is a dead man, and that leaves the two of us to face them. But I'm getting out. Are you coming, or are you going to stay here and wait for them to come get you?"

He was already in the saddle when she swung up beside him. They drove in the spurs and loped away into the night, leaving death and silence behind them. Silence except for the rest of the horses galloping away into the darkness. Wallace had seen to that.

Chapter 20

AS FOR Nino, he had spent a very pleasant day. One of the White Eyes had killed himself far away down there in the desert when they had come up from behind and surprised him. That made one of the party. This morning they had attacked the others and captured a second. That made two. A third had tried to escape into the night and run right into two of his warriors. That made three. Nino had sat there in the darkness with his dark back against the bole of a tree and counted them off on his fingers for the dozenth time and grinned to himself. While the Grumbler and three of the younger warriors had thrown the captive with the hairy face over a saddle and carried him away into the night, Nino had continued to sit there and send out his thought spirits to Poco.

He taunted him, he told him they had no water and that he and his men had plenty of time, he gloated over what Poco would think on the following morning when he saw the head of his friend sticking up out of the ground at the base of an anthill not far from the rocks that now were their prison; not far from where the two of them had talked.

But he was totally unprepared for the four faint reports of a pistol when they came from far away out there; out in the direction where the Grumbler and the three others had taken the captive. He let out a screech to the warrior with him and leaped to his feet. The single rope rein of his pony was tethered to Nino's wrist and he hit the saddle in a lithe-legged bound. With the warrior close behind him, he drove his pony through the night toward where the shots had come. He heard his warriors yelling and some vague sixth sense told him that something was wrong.

He even heard firing from up among the rock cluster and thought that it was the White Eyes shooting at his warriors in the night. His horse was heaving hard as he finally saw outlines, sent out a signal call, and pulled up by the ant mound.

Four or five of his last remaining men sat in a circle on their ponies and said nothing. He could tell, even in the darkness, that there was death in the air. He swung down and strode over and almost stepped on the body of the Grumbler. From nearby came two more horses, and the sentinels to the east pulled up.

"We killed one of them," they cried out excitedly. "He tried to run away but almost ran on top of us up close by the rocks. But he was only a Me-hi-cano. One of those who fled today when we came."

They were excited, elated; they had something to boast about when the party returned to their main camp far away to the north. But Nino paid them no attention.

"You saw nobody?" he demanded.

A warrior spoke up. "One man. He came by close to us, riding like the hawk flies. He shot once and sent one of our warriors to the abode."

Nino stood there for a moment and then went slowly to his horse. He swung up into the rawhide saddle.

"It was Poco," he said. "Nobody but Poco would have done it."

"Two of the White Eyes ran away," said another. "We heard them but were too far away."

"Poco," Nino said again, his eyes burning in the darkness. "We will wait no longer. We will go in and kill them all. Then I will catch Poco and for three days I will run burning slivers into his breast and cut away his eyelids that the sun may shine into them. . . ."

He drove in his heels and they followed him without hesitation. Straight toward that cluster of rocks they drove at a run. Two of the men were those who had killed Lopez the bandit. One rode the horse with which he had tried to escape. In its two saddle bags were two canvas bags filled with green-colored paper; green on one side and gold-colored on the other.

They drove straight up to the rocks and jumped down and were in among them almost in a flash, guns, knives, lances and throwing axes ready. The fire still burned brightly, and in its light and the silence Nino paused to look about him.

One White Eyes, a small one with a pipe stem clenched tightly between his fingers, sat slumped against a rock as though asleep. There were two spots of blood on the front of his shirt. Another, a man as big as a fat squaw, lay flat on his back. There was nothing else to greet them.

No live ones, no horses. Nothing but two dead men, the silence of death, and a fire that already was beginning to die down. Nino turned and strode back to his horse.

"This is a place of evil," he said. "We must get away from here and follow the trails of the others."

"But the night is dark and our ghosts are abroad, those from the abode," protested one of the others. "Many of our horses are loose and there are those to be buried."

"The Me-hi-canos we chased away will return and take care of the horses after we are gone. We will send out thought spirits to the ghosts of those abroad."

He made no mention of the dead lying out there. The rage in him was too great. Poco had said that men without eyes could not see to pour water. And now there was no time for the dead. Poco had been right. There would be no water poured out on the ground while Poco's tongue was burned by the sun.

Nino led a saddened, silent band of warriors out of there that night. They had to go at a walk, for two of them were down on foot, bending low over the ground, following the tracks of the two horses. Their horses were being led. They followed the tracks in the night for more than three miles. Here they had turned from a northwesterly direction and were heading due west; down out of the hills and toward the desert below.

"It's as I thought," Nino told his men, some eight or nine in number now. "The woman with the yellow hair and one of the White Eyes are heading for the big hacienda down there in the desert miles away. Come."

He turned off to the left and gigged his pony into a lope, the others following. It has been said that an Apache could get more speed and distance out of a horse than any rider that ever lived. They drove it to the point of exhaustion and then, cruelly, forced it to go on until it dropped from under them. They drove the ponies now, down through the timber and ran them across the open spaces. The terrain fell away, down the long slopes, and the hours passed.

They came at last to the foot of the great escarpment, having cut a long circle to get around their quarry. Now they swung to the north again for two miles. Here Nino strung out his men for another mile and a half.

They dropped from their tired ponies and waited.

They did not have long to wait. Not more than a half-hour later sounds came from somewhere high above on the slope and among the trees. The coyote signals began to go out and the warriors hurriedly converged at a spot from which the sounds were coming. All were dismounted now; lean, lithe-legged figures that blended with the darkness. They followed the downward progress of the two riders and moved over to intercept them.

Finally a tired horse broke through into an opening. Wallace was in the lead. Close behind him came the woman. As they reached the last fringe of trees Wallace turned in the saddle.

"We're in the clear, Gert. They can't pick up our tracks until daylight, and by that time—"

Something leaped at his horse, and in the lightning second that he first saw it, became aware of it, and tried to reach for a gun, he thought it was what the plains people called a catamount. It struck the side of his horse just as three others did. Fingers of steel grabbed his arm and he felt himself yanked from the saddle and smothered under snarling bodies. He heard the woman scream, and then a blow struck him on the head and he knew no more.

He came out of it to find a fire going nearby. He was bound hand and foot, trussed up on the ground, and so was the woman. Nino stood before the fire, and when he saw that Wallace had come to he stepped over and kicked him in the face with a moccasined foot.

"You and the woman will die," Nino said. "You will pay for those of my warriors you White Eyes have sent to the abode."

Wallace grunted with pain and disdain. He couldn't understand a word of what the foul-smelling devil was saying, but the implication was clear. But one thing could be said of the man, black-souled though he was: he had courage.

He looked over at the woman and grinned. "What an end to a beautiful romance, Gert."

"No talk," snarled one of the warriors, speaking most of the English words he knew.

Nino said something to one of the others, a middle-aged warrior, who stepped forward. He grinned down at Wallace.

"Me one time scout White Eyes soldiers. You die strong."

Nino stood there looking at the woman. She stared back at him. Her face was a little blanched but that was all. Her lips were firm. He stepped over and bent down and ran his dark hands through the long braid of yellow hair entwined around her head. They came free when he pulled at them, and he sat down and began to unplait them. From the warriors came little hissing intakes of breath that told of inner excitement.

The ex-scout grinned down at her. "Yellow hair. Burn good," he said.

Nino straightened, letting her hair fall to the ground. He nodded toward Wallace. "Poco can not find us until tomorrow, and then he will trail us here. These will die and then we'll wait for him. Tie the White Eyes to a tree."

It was then that the shot came, the booming roar of a .45-70 Sharps single shot came from not too far away. Something struck Nino in front so hard that it knocked him down and then rolled him over twice. He came to a motionless heap flat down on his face, crimson beginning to work from his dark-skinned body. It glowed eerily in the light of the fire. The warriors took one look at the fallen figure, and then panic ensued.

Normally an Apache didn't stampede. When ambush came they always, from instinct, reacted automatically and were gone in a flash. Then they fled. It had even happened in the big battle of Apache Pass when Mangas Colorados—Red Sleeves—and two hundred of his warriors had ambushed a large body of soldiers and penned them in for a wipeout. But one fleeing soldier, whose horse had been shot from under him and had warriors closing in for the kill, had taken a long range shot at a big Indian and knocked him off his horse. In a matter of minutes the fight was over, the Apaches fleeing.

It happened that night at the foot of the Sierra Madre where the desert came up to meet the great Mother Mountain. Nino's warriors fled on foot, and two minutes later the sound of their running horses came from below as they fled into the desert, back toward the American line, back to tell the others that Nino had gone to the abode.

Presently, as Wallace and the woman lay there in silence, there came a footstep from nearby and a tall figure in moccasins stepped into the firelight.

"Cogin!" she cried out. "Cogin, thank God you got here in time. They said they were going to work on us and must have thought you wouldn't be here until morning."

"We had a little ruckus out there where they were burying One-Card in an ant mound so we could see him at daylight. There were four of them covering him when I slipped up on the other side. Three never knew what hit them, they were so busy. The fourth was the one that yelled."

"We heard the shots," Wallace said.

"I grabbed an Indian pony, one belonging to one of the four, and started for the rocks. But a warrior ran close by, so I got in a lucky shot," he said simply. "I went back a ways and waited for Nino. When he charged the rocks and found nothing, I figgered something was wrong. I took a look inside, Wallace," he added.

"He shot them both, Charley," she said in a tight, level voice. "He did it to force me to come with him or stay there and burn."

"So I figured," he answered, and bent over her with the knife. He cut her bonds and she got slowly to her feet, a little stiff.

"Charley," she asked him, her eyes searching his face, "what happened to poor One-Card?"

"One of the Indians shot him when Nino came," he said simply.

She thought, looking at his lean, unshaved face: I think you're lying, but if you are I'm glad you didn't tell me.

He went over and rolled Nino over on his back. Wallace said from where he was still trussed up, "I'm glad you killed that murdering devil."

"All depends upon how you look upon a killing a man," Cogin grunted. "And I didn't kill him. I put one through his shoulder to knock him down and out. I knew his men would run for it. I'm taking him back alive."

Dawn broke over the little camp, if such it could be called. It found Nino, bandaged from strips torn from the woman's underskirt, lying beside the fire. He was conscious now, and you could see in his eyes the dregs of defeat, the shame, the undying humiliation at what his hated enemy had done to him. He had been glad when the White Eyes had taken Poco away and thus reopened Nino's path to Keneta's *jacal* with his horess. And now . . . he closed his eyes to shut out the sight of him, to send out pleading thought spirits at his terrible failure.

"What are you going to do with me, Charley?" Wallace asked, only his hands tied back of him now. "You trailed me a good many hundred miles to kill me. What's it going to be—murder while I'm tied or an even break?"

Cogin shook his head. "Neither one, Wallace. You and I think a little different along those lines. You'll end up in Kansas in front of a jury. You'll hang."

"And your friend the Apache?" sneered the murderer.

"He won't be much good for raiding any more after what that slug did to his shoulder bones. I'm going to use him to try to make peace with the bigger fellows."

He turned and went back to the fire, and the eyes of the woman followed him.

Some three weeks later Cogin and the woman known as Gert rode slowly up the creek toward the little settlement. It was late afternoon and comparatively cool beneath the cottonwoods. The birds were chirping and carrying on their mock battles, and there was a buzzard or two still sailing around. Cogin had met a patrol of soldiers two days before and had turned over his two prisoners to the army, Wallace to be sent back to Kansas under guard to stand trial for the murder of Cogin's sister. If a death verdict failed there, the officer had agreed to see that he would be held for the murder of the cashiers of the two banks he had robbed. Nino had promised Cogin that the money would be returned.

There had been silence between him and the woman for quite some time now. During the time they had stayed at a big hacienda to rest up and let Nino recover somewhat, his manner toward her had not changed. Now she shot him a sidewise glance, moving up beside him. The packhorse they had secured in Mexico plodded along on its lead rope.

"My place is just up beyond that next big group of trees and not far from the settlement," she said. "If you'd care to stop off long enough I'll cook you a good supper. I owe you that much for changing a few things in my life."

He said, "Are you going back to the pack train work?"

She shook her head. "I'm going back to Texas. I can

get enough for my mules and equipment, and I've a little hidden at the place. Hornbuckle was right about staying too long in one place and then it being too late to make a fresh start. I'm making that fresh start."

They came to the trees and he saw a comfortable adobe cabin with corrals and sheds out back. The front door was open, the corrals empty. It had an air of desertion about it.

"That's strange," she said. "I told those packers to stay here until I got back."

They loped up to the place and swung down and went inside. It was in shambles, the furniture smashed, the kitchen wrecked. A big wood rat ran halfway across the floor, paused to eye them beadily, and then scurried away.

"At a first-hand guess," he said wryly, but smiling a little, "I'd say that your boys decided to go into business for themselves. They took the whole outfit and burned the breeze for Mexico."

She surprised him by smiling right back. "That saves me a lot of time and bother, Charley. Wait until I get a few handfuls of money I have hidden and I'll buy your supper instead of cooking it."

He went out and mounted, and presently she reappeared and swung up. They jogged on up the broad trail for about two hundred yards and then pulled up sharply and stared down. Off to one side of the trail were five fresh mounds of earth. A few feet away was a giant cottonwood with big spreading limbs. Both looked up instinctively.

"Come on!" she cried out. "There's something wrong around here!"

They drove forward at a gallop, the pack horse thumping along behind, and in a matter of minutes the settlement came into view. It was deserted, not a soul in sight. Cogin swung down before the place where the Mexican woman had served him the food. It was as though she had simply walked out and left everything. The cow and calf were together in the shade of a cottonwood and there wasn't a chicken in sight. Coyotes.

"She wanted to go back to Mexico," Cogin told the woman. "It looks like the packers took her back."

She turned from a few feet away and beckoned to him. He strode over and peered inside one of the rooms where two of the outlaws had lived. The place was pock-marked by bullet holes and on one spot on the dirt floor there was a dried crust of what had been crimson.

It was the same in the other places. Hornbuckle's bar was in shambles.

He said quietly, "Posse. Looks like they barreled in here after some badly wanted men and decided to clean out the whole place. Well, they did a good job."

"Yes, Charley, they did a good job," she said slowly. "One that was long overdue. And if Limpy and One-Card and Bart and Horn . . . and Gert the smuggler had been here instead of in Mexico . . ." She left the rest of it unsaid.

He leaned his back against an adobe wall with the fresh pockmarks in it and rolled a cigarette. He lit it and let the match drop between his spurred boots, and from long habit in the grassy range country where fires can prove disastrous, he rubbed it out with his boot. The spur rattled oddly.

Finally he said, "Well, I guess I'd better be getting along. I'm due at the fort this week to see Nino and the officers. I'll have to tell old Tacana that I killed his brother, but I don't think the wrinkled old devil will mind a great deal."

She laughed, a little strangely. "Yes, it's funny how things work out. We went after 'bounty money' and only one of us got back alive. And if we had all remained here things probably would have come out the same way. One-Card would have said it was in the cards. I guess so. If the Apaches hadn't got you, you'd have been just like other people instead of what you are. And if I hadn't met a very right man in some ways but a very wrong man in a lot of other ways, we wouldn't be two of a kind."

"I hadn't thought about it that way," he said thoughtfully, "not until now. Do you reckon, Gert—"

"Yes," she said, and stepped over, and despite her tallness she had to look up at him. "Yes, I reckon, Charley. Two of an odd kind might make one of the right kind."

"I was sort of thinking the same thing," he answered, and felt an odd feeling go through him. He dropped the cigarette. "We'll talk it over on the way to the fort. Well, we'd better get going. Nino will be waiting. He's kind of anxious for me to see what Keneta and those three little Apaches look like."